Stacy Yeh
Joanna Yang ◎著

GROUND CREW ENGLIS

航空地勤職場口語英文

地勤工作的在職觀察報告，告別職場菜英文！

強力推薦給：
各航空系大學生
地勤求職新鮮人
地勤從業人員

- 職場實境對話，與旅客英文對談不慌張！
- 母語人士常用句型，丟掉中式英文句子！
- 字彙片語解析，搞懂工作常用的單字片語！
- 學長姐經驗談，入行前先知道地勤在幹嘛！

收錄【櫃台】、【出境】、【入境】、【特殊狀況處理】四大工作情境：
行李超重要加錢？機位超賣客人發飆？班機又延誤了？
地勤前輩教你工作碰到以上這些狀況時該怎麼辦？！

MP3

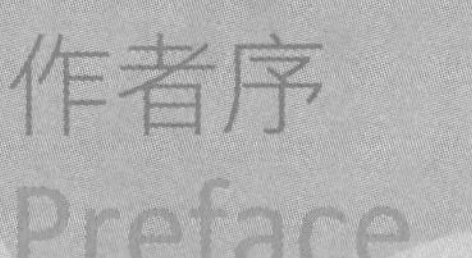

作者序 Preface

一般人對於航空公司地勤人員的印象，就只是單純負責旅客劃位和托運行李，看似輕鬆簡單的工作內容。然而，自己真正踏入航空業後，發現擔任地勤一職著實不易，需要具備耐心與細心去注意許多細節，例如：各國簽証、托運行李限額和特殊行李的處理方式、旅客需求特別協助的安排、機位超賣、班機延誤或取消等。

此書透過39個實境對話、中英文對照、職場經驗分享，不僅讓讀者們學習到航空公司的英文專業用語，也能得知在面對不同狀況時地勤人員如何妥善處理安排。希望藉由此書讓對於航空業有興趣的人能夠一窺究竟，並具有專業工作知識。

Joanna Yang

作者序
Preface

我真的從小沒想過會當地勤，也沒想過教人家英文，更沒想過會出書。沒想到一下子三件事一次到齊了。既然有這機會，就來談進入航空公司這回事吧。

很多人期盼進入航空業，不論是地勤或是空服，甚至有人開了補習班，專門教你進入航空業。其中很重要的一環就是「英文」這一關。不論本土或外商航空，一定要求基本的英文能力，誰叫英文還是世界強勢語言？很多人會有一種迷思，覺得英文越好越容易被航空公司選上。答案是「是」也「不是」。英文是一個必要條件，只要達到一定水準，能簡單明瞭與人溝通、能閱讀一般公司的說明及規定即可。據我自己的觀察其他尚有許多特質，更是航空公司青睞的：平易近人、熱心、耐心、為他人著想等外，最重要的是「同理心」。而「同理心」必須透過語言及行動表達才會完整，因此英文越好越容易被選上嗎？是，也不是。

本書內容以實際情境的對話為主，不會有太艱澀的內容。因為在實際工作時，能完整表達才是重點，而不是困難的生字或拗口的語法。本書不僅帶欲從事航空業者一探究竟，常出國旅行的讀者也能從中得知為什麼在機場要經過這麼多手續。同時，我們以自身工作經驗，提供讀者一探地勤工作的真實血淚，並學習生活、旅行中實用的英語。

Stacy Yeh

目次 Contents

1 Part 櫃台

2 Part 出境

Part 3 入境

Part 4 特殊狀況處理

Part 1 櫃台

1-1 Briefing

情境介紹

一天早上開櫃台前，督導 Lily 集合所有早班同仁，簡單報告當天上午各班飛機的狀況。

情境對話 Track 01

L ▸ Lily

L: Good morning, everyone. There are 3 flights this morning, XX451 to Tokyo, XX453 to Hong Kong, and XX 437 to Bangkok. 182 passengers will take the first flight XX451. 5 of them fly business class, and 177 of them fly economy class.

There will be 1 infant and 1 pre-ordered wheelchair. Both are in the economy class, so it is possible to have a baby stroller. Additionally, 3 vegetarian meals needed in total. 1 is for business class and the other 2 are for the economy class. Besides, there is 1 diabetic meal for a diabetic passenger in business class which I have already noted in the system, please be aware of it.

158 passengers will take the second flight XX453. 3 of them sit in business class, and 155 of them sit in economy class. There will be 20 group guests transit in Hong Kong.

Their final destination is Geneva. One of the group guests has no passport information in the system so please ask for it before checking in.

The third flight XX437 will be delayed for 40 minutes.12 passengers have ongoing flights, and 8 of them will connect with XX251 to London. As the scheduled time of XX251 is 16:10, they might not catch this flight, please transfer them to the next flight to London XX253. The other 4 are going to Chingmai by other airlines that we are unable to change their booking, but I have confirmed the time of their ongoing flight which will be delayed for 2 hours. There's no need to worry about it.

Finally, please don't forget to provide the best manner of service.

譯文

L: 各位，早安。今天早上有三班飛機，分別為 XX451 飛往東京、XX453 飛往香港以及 XX437 飛往曼谷。

第一班飛機 XX451 有 182 位旅客，有 5 位在商務艙、177 位在經濟艙。這班飛機將有一位嬰兒和一個事先預約的輪椅，兩位乘客都在經濟艙，所以可能會有一部嬰兒車。此外，共有三份素食餐，一份在商務艙，而另外兩份在經濟艙。還有一份糖尿病飲食餐是給一位商務艙乘客，我已經在系統裡註記，請特別留意。

第二班飛機 XX453 有 158 位乘客，有 3 位在商務艙、155 位在經濟艙，經濟艙有一團 20 名成員的團體客人，會在香港轉機。他們的目的地是日內瓦。其中一名團員在系統裡沒有護照資料，所以在辦理登機前先跟他們要。

第三班飛機 XX437 將會延遲 40 分鐘，而有 12 位乘客還要接下一班飛機。其中 8 位要接 XX251 往倫敦。因為 XX251 表定時間是 16:10，所以他們可能接不上這班飛機，請將他們轉到下一班往倫敦的 XX253。另外 4 位需轉機的乘客是搭乘外家航空前往清邁，我們無法變更他們的訂位紀錄，但我已經確認這班飛機將會延遲 2 小時。他們無需擔心。

最後，請別忘了拿出最優質的服務態度。

英文母語者這麼說

There will be 1 infant and 1 pre-order wheelchair. Both are in economy class, so it is possible to have a baby stroller.（因為這班飛機將有一位嬰兒和一個事先預約的輪椅，兩位乘客都在經濟艙，所以可能會有一部嬰兒車。）

在這裡要提到中文的「因為…所以…」的句型。在中文裡，我們習慣把「因為」跟「所以」都一起放在句子中。但是在英文裡，如果說了 because 就不用 so；反之，句子裡已經有 so 前面就不會有 because。因此，請不要說 *Because there will be 1 infant and 1 pre-order wheelchair, ..., so it is possible to have a baby stroller*，中間的 *both are in economy class* 是補充說明前面的 *1 infant and 1 pre-order wheelchair* 這兩位乘客，如果覺得句子好長，先忽略掉它會比較容易懂。

另一句話也是一樣的用法：

"As the scheduled time of XX251 is 16:10, they might not catch this flight, please transfer them to the next flight to London XX253."

在這裡 as 也是為「因為」使用，因此用了 as 就不再使用 so 了。

字彙解析

- **passenger** *n.* 旅客

  Passengers are trapped due to the typhoon.（旅客們因為颱風被困住了。）

- **wheelchair** *n.* 輪椅

  The wheelchair is broken.（那把輪椅壞掉了。）

- **economy class** 經濟艙

  Passengers fly with the economy class are much more than business class.（搭經濟艙的旅客遠比搭商務艙多。）

- **business class** 商務艙

  You can take a rest in the Lounge if you fly with the business class.（如果你搭商務艙，可以到貴賓室休息一下。）

- **diabetic meal** 糖尿病飲食餐，含豐富碳水化合物、高纖維、低脂肪及卡路里。此種餐膳適用於不論是否需要依賴胰島素的糖尿病人。

  I would like to order a diabetic meal for my grandfather.（我想幫我外公訂一份糖尿病飲食餐。）

- **transit** *v.* 轉機

  She will make a transit in Frankfurt.（她會在法蘭克福轉機。）

- **delay** *v.* 延遲

  My flight was delayed, so I couldn't attend the meeting.（我的飛機延遲所以我沒辦法參加那個會議。）

補充片語

❶ be aware of 意識到；注意、留意

例 I have been aware of that suspicious guy for a while.（我已經注意到那可疑的男子一陣子了。）

解 be aware of 有「覺察」的意思，含有要多留意、費點心思的意涵。

❷ ask for 要求某事物

例 He asked for help but everyone ignored him.（他請求幫助但每個人都不理他。）

解 使用 ask for 表示説話一方放低身段，用較客氣的態度請求他人做什麼事或給予物品。

❸ be unable to 沒辦法、無法

例 The internet was disconnected, so I was unable to log in.（網路斷線所以我沒辦法登入。）

解 be unable to 幾乎與 cannot、can't 意思很相近，但還是有些許不同。cannot、can't 是「沒有能力去做」，比如説 I can't swim.；而 be unable to 則是「有能力，但因外界因素而無法」的意思。因此如果説 I was unable to swim 應該是有什麼原因讓我不能游泳了。

In Other Words

❶ Their final destination is Geneva. = They will arrive at Geneva in the end.（他們的目的地是日內瓦。）

解 in the end 是「最後」的意思，也可以用 at last 代替。「他們的目的地是日內瓦」，也就是說「他們最後會抵達日內瓦」。「抵達」arrive 常用 at 來連接地方名稱。

❷ One of the group guests has no passport information in the system so please ask for it before checking in. = One of the group guests doesn't have passport information in the system so please ask for it before checking in.（其中一名團員在系統裡沒有護照資料，所以在辦理登機前先跟他們要。）

解 在中文裡我們說「沒有」，英文可有兩種說法，即 have／has no 或是說 don't／doesn't have，兩者是相通的。

地勤工作解說

每天上櫃台之前，都會由當班督導跟所有同事報告今天航班的狀況。如果有特殊情況，會先讓同事知道，比方上述情境督導已事先得知第三班飛機會延遲 40 分鐘，就事先做好對策有些人要轉下一班飛機，對外說法都一致，才會讓客人覺得航班沒問題。

前輩經驗巧巧說

各機場、各公司上櫃檯的時間不一定，因有些機場有宵禁（通常較小的機場都有），晚上 12 點過後就沒有飛機起降，因此早班同事有固定上櫃台的時間。通常在一開始會由當班督導將航班資訊告知同事。除了上述航班延遲的情形外，其他如某些國家改變了簽證或過境規定、某些國家的某航空公司正在罷工及會有什麼影響、天氣狀況如颱風來襲航班有異動等，都會在這個時間讓同事了解，面對客人時才能夠回答或作處理。

1-2 機場櫃台劃位報到

情境介紹

一位台灣商務人士直飛上海浦東機場，一般櫃台的標準劃位流程。

情境對話 Track 02

A ▸ Alice，B ▸ Business Man

A: Good evening, Sir. Where is your final destination today?

B: I am going to ShangHai.

A: Your passport, Taiwan Compatriot Pass and itinerary, please.

B: Here. Oh, I am going to Pudong, not Hongqiao.

A: Okay, let me check your visa endorsement first... okay. And... yes, you're taking XX892 flight from Hong Kong to Pudong Airport. May I confirm with you that you have ordered a vegetarian raw meal, all fruits and vegetables along with pure fruit or vegetable juices?

B: That's right. I just went to our annual employee health examination, and there were some red numbers in the result so my wife warned me to eat more vegetables. Huh.

A: Please take care. Any baggage to check in?

B: Yes, please.

A: Okay... it is 14 kg. Please refer to the sheet. Any restricted items inside?

B: No.

A: Thank you. Here is your baggage reciept, Hong Kong to Pudong, Shanghai.

B: Okay.

A: Would you like to have a window seat or an aisle seat?

B: An aisle seat, please. In the front if possible, thank you.

A: Sure. I believe you need a quiet place before working.

B: Thank you.

A: Okay, here are your passport, Taiwan Compatriot Pass and boarding pass. Please board at gate 42. The seat is 35C which is an aisle seat. Please stand in line waiting for baggage check at the terminal counter. Have a nice flight.

B: That's great, thank you.

譯文

A: 先生，晚安。請問您今天目的地是哪裡？

B: 我要去上海。

A: 麻煩您的護照、台胞證及行程表。

B: 在這。喔對，我要去浦東，不是虹橋。

A: 好的，先讓我確認一下您的台胞證加簽…好了。然後是，您搭乘 XX892 從香港飛往浦東機場。可以跟您確認一下，您是否訂了一個全素餐，是僅提供水果及蔬菜搭配純鮮果汁的？

B: 沒錯。我剛做了年度員工體檢，結果有一些紅字在報告上，所以我太太警告我要多吃蔬菜。哼。

A: 請您多保重。有任何行李要托運嗎？

B: 有，麻煩你。

A: 好的…14 公斤。麻煩請參考這張單子，有任何違禁品在裡面嗎？

B: 沒有。

A: 謝謝。這是您的行李收據，香港到上海浦東。

B: 好的。

A: 請問您想要靠窗的座位，還是走道邊的座位？

B: 請給我走道的座位。如果可以的話最好在前面一點，謝謝。

A: 當然。我相信您工作前需要一個安靜的位置。

B: 謝謝。

A: 好的，這裡是您的護照、台胞證及登機證。請於 42 號門登機。座位在 35C，是靠走道的座位。請在這排櫃台末端等候行李檢查。祝您有個愉快的旅程。

B: 太好了，謝謝。

英文母語者這麼說

Your passport, Taiwan Compatriot Pass and itinerary, please.

（請（給我）您的護照、台胞證及行程表。）

中文我們請人家給我們東西，會直接說出「請給我～」，但在英文裡常會省略「給」這個動作，另一方面，"Please give me ～"好像太直接了，所以口語上，直接說出你要什麼東西就可以了。

Would you like to have a window seat or an aisle seat?

（請問您想要靠窗的座位或是走道座位？）

請不要說"Do you want to have a window seat or an aisle seat?"這聽起比較不客氣。"Do you want～"也是「你想要」的意思沒錯，但通常是對很熟的人才會用這麼直接的語氣，建議用"Would you like～"比較好。簡單說，這兩者就像是在中文裡加上「請問」及沒有加的差別。

字彙解析

- **business man**　商務人士

  This course is for business men only.（這個課程僅提供給商務人士的。）

- **passport** *n.*　護照

  You can't travel abroad without passport.（你沒有護照不能出國旅行。）

- **Taiwan Compatriot Pass**　台胞證

  All Taiwanese need to apply Taiwan Compatriot Pass as a travel permit to go to China.（台灣人要去中國的話都要申請被視為旅行許可的台胞證。）

- **visa endorsement**　加簽（台胞證）

  Having visa endorsement is a must before going to China.（去中國之前一定要先辦（台胞證）加簽。）

- **annual employee health examination**　年度員工體檢

  Our company provides annual on employee health examination.（我們公司有提供年度員工體檢。）

- **aisle** *n.*　走道

  There is no aisle seat.（已經沒有走道的座位了。）

補充片語

❶ Huh 嘿；哈，用來表示疑問、驚奇或蔑視

解 像是一個發語詞，像台灣人會用「蛤」這種本身沒有意思的字來表示情緒的詞一樣。文中商務人士則是被老婆要求多吃菜，也只能 Huh 一聲表示抗議（但還是乖乖照做了）。

❷ refer to 參考、參閱

例 Please refer to our instruction before you start the lesson.（在課程開始前，請參考我們的說明。）

解 refer to 有「提到」的意思，但在本篇，則為「參考」、「參閱」的意思，也蠻常在一些說明會、指導語中出現。

❸ if possible 如果可以的話

例 May I have an extra day off this Friday if possible?（如果可以的話，我這星期五可以多休一天嗎？）

解 if possible 作為副詞，口語上可以放在句首、句中、句尾，你想到要補充說明「如果可以的話」的地方都可以，有種「不勉強」的意味在。

In Other Words

❶ Where is your final destination today? = May I have your destination today?（請問您今天的目的地是哪裡？）

解 最普遍的說法還是原句 where is your final destination today，但在這裏提供一個很常用的 May I 開頭的句子，使用這個開頭都帶有「尊敬」的意思，服務業常會用到，尤其有時候遇到較害羞的客人，對方沒有開口要求協助的時候，想要主動去協助的話，也可以用這個開頭，侵略性比較不會那麼強，聽者也比較舒服一點。

❷ Would you like to have a window seat or an aisle seat? = Which one do you prefer? A window seat or an aisle seat?（您想要靠窗座位還是走道座位？）

解 當有兩個選項可以選擇的時候，可以用 which 開頭詢問對方，想要 A 還是要 B。如上述要詢問客人想要窗口或是走道的座位，可以用 Would you like a window seat or an aisle seat 也可以拆成兩句變成 Which one do you prefer? A window seat or an aisle seat?

地勤工作解說

這一篇是最單純的辦理登機標準流程。客人很配合，文件、簽證、行李等都備齊，目的地又是很常見的地方，遇到這樣的客人是最「方便」的了。如果順利的話，其實 check in 一位客人很迅速，大約 2～3 分鐘就可以結束。若是遇到票有問題、行李超重、簽證沒辦…等，只要一個環節都會拖累 check in 的速度，有時候甚至無法辦理登機。

前輩經驗巧巧說

辦理登機的流程如下：先向客人詢問目的地，收取護照，確認訂位系統裡有該客人的訂位記錄，電子機票有連上，再查詢以該客人的國籍身份，到他的目的地是否需要簽證？或是有特殊的相關規定？以上沒有問題的話就可以為客人秤行李重量，詢問是否攜帶違禁品？沒有問題就可以出行李條，與客人確認行李條的目的地無誤，最後出登機證，再次確認登機證與護照上的姓名拼音相符合，就可以將護照及登機證一併交給客人，請客人稍等後行李檢查，就完成啦！

1–3 頭等櫃台

情境介紹

一位頭等艙乘客於香港專機前往雪梨，帶了三件行李。

情境對話 Track 03

I ▸ Iris，B ▸ Mr. Barclays

I: Good evening, Sir. Where is your final destination today?

B: Sydney.

I: May I have your passport and itinerary, please?

B: Here.

I: Thank you, Mr. Barclays. May I confirm with you... you are traveling to Sydney via Hong Kong with the first class all the way?

B: That's right.

I: Okay. Do you have any checked baggage?

B: Yes. A lot. Here.

I: How many pieces do you have?

B: 3 in total.

I: Please lay them down and watch the carousel. Thank you.

B: Okay.

I: Oh, excuse me, Mr. Barclays. The limitation of one baggage is 32kg, and this baggage is 34kg. Would you please adjust a little bit? It's for safety.

B: Really? Alright. This is my very first time hearing that there is a limitation.

I: Thank you, Sir. The priority tags are attached on your baggage.

B: Will baggage with this bag be sent faster?

I: Yes. They will be settled at the place close to the door.

B: Great.

I: And here are your baggage receipts and boarding pass. Please keep them carefully. And here is your lounge invitation. Please enjoy it.

B: Where is the lounge?

I: It is in the Southern wing. You will see it on your right hand side after going through the immigration.

B: Okay. Thank you.

I: Thank you, Mr. Barclays. Have a nice flight.

譯文

I: 先生，晚安。請問今天您的目的地是哪裡呢？

B: 雪梨。

I: 請給我您的護照及行程。

B: 在這。

I: 謝謝您，Barclays 先生。先讓我跟您確認，您今天是在香港轉機到雪梨，全程都搭乘頭等艙。

B: 沒錯。

I: 好的。請問您有要托運的行李嗎？

B: 有，很多。在這。

I: 請問有幾件呢？

B: 總共三件。

I: 請將他們躺放在輸送帶上，謝謝。

B: 好。

I: 噢，不好意思，Barclays 先生。我們每件行李最多是 32 公斤，這件行李是 34 公斤。您可以稍微調整一下嗎？這是為了安全起見。

B: 是嗎？好吧。這是我第一次聽說有這個限制。

I: 謝謝您，先生。優先領取行李的掛牌已經幫您掛上了。

B: 掛那牌子的行李是會送快一點嗎？

I: 是的。我們會將它們放在靠近艙門的地方。

B: 很好。

I: 然後這是您的行李收據及登機證，請小心收好。再來這是您的貴賓室邀請卡。請您享用。

B: 你們貴賓室在哪裡？

I: 在南翼。您過關之後就可以看到它在您右手邊。

B: 好的，謝謝。

I: 謝謝您，Barclays 先生。祝您有個美好的旅程。

英文母語者這麼說

This is my very first time hearing that there is a limitation.

（這還是我第一次聽說有限制。）

這個說法蠻常見到用在英文中，因此提出來說明。在 first 前面加上 the very（這裏是用 my 取代了 the），其實這裏的 very 沒有意思，僅代表加強語氣罷了，因此不要翻成「非常」。所以整句可翻譯成「這還是我第一次聽說有限制」，帶有強調「第一次聽說」這件事情。不要因為中文裡有「還」就用了 still，意思不太一樣唷。

字彙解析

- **extra** *adj.* 額外的

  This extra service is free.（這額外的服務是免費的。）

- **lay** *v.* 放、擱

  Please lay the sheet on the table.（請把那張單子放在桌上。）

- **adjust** *v.* 調整

  He adjusts the machine every week.（他每個禮拜調整一次機器。）

- **safety** *n.* 安全

This is for your safety.（這是為了你的安全。）

- **priority** *n.* 優先、在先

Passengers with infants have priority to enter to the cabin.（嬰兒隨行的乘客有提前進入機艙的優先權。）

補充片語

❶ all the way 全程

例 He slept on the plane all the way.（他在飛機上全程都在睡覺。）

解 表示從開始到結束，都在做同一件事情。

❷ lay down 躺下來；放在地上

例 You can lay the bag down here.（你可以把包包放下來。）

解 lay down 有很多種意思，這裏單純指的是放在地上、把東西躺著放下來的意思。

In Other Words

❶ The priority tags are attached on your baggages. = Your baggages are tagged with priority tags.（已經將優先領取的標籤掛在您的行李上了。）

解 可以說「優先領取標籤已經附在您的行李上了」，或是「（已經

為）您的行李已經掛上優先領取標籤了」，只是主語、受語的不同而已。

地勤工作解說

頭等艙的客人是最重要的一群人。就算他是其他航空公司的會員，只是這次因為某些因素搭了另一家航空，也會得到最高的禮遇。因為負擔得起頭等艙的客人都是潛力股。有可能因為這一次美好的搭乘經驗讓他往後選擇其他航空，甚至可能因此他整個公司的差旅交通都會因此改搭此航空。難怪頭等艙乘客總是貴賓了。

前輩經驗巧巧說

在這裡先說明，其實不是每一架飛機都有頭等艙！飛機有不同機型，通常要大飛機才有頭等艙，但也不是每一架都有，要看機型及其內裝，許多飛機是只有商務艙及經濟艙的。一般來說，頭等艙是最高級的，再來是商務艙，再來是經濟艙。通常有能力搭乘頭等艙或商務艙的客人，都是有一定影響力的人。如同上述所說，都是潛力股，可能他平常搭的不是你們家的飛機，可能是別家的常客，但這次因為某些原因來搭你們家了，這不正是主動送上門推銷的好機會嗎？如果這次搭乘經驗讓他感到非常滿意，甚至勝過原東家，那就是搶到一個大客戶了。尤其這些客人可能是公司老闆、經理等握有決定權的人，可能因此將整個公司的生意都給你們做了，當然要好好表現。航空業也是很現實的！

1-4 會員櫃台

情境介紹

一位剛剛加入 Sunshine 航空公司飛行常客計畫的客人，還不是很清楚會員有哪些禮遇，櫃檯主動說明。

情境對話 Track 04

R ▸ Rita，Y ▸ **Mr. Yang**

Y: Excuse me, I have some questions about the membership because I just joined your frequent flyer club. I was wondering if there is any difference between this club and another airline club I joined earlier, in case I cross the line.

R: Sure! I am glad to help.

Y: Thank you. I am confused about the baggage limit. How much is it?

R: I understand. This is sometimes confusing. Let me explain it for you, Mr. Yang. You just joined our frequent flyers, which means you are now a green card member. When you earn 30,000 miles, you'll become a silver member. Moreover, there is a gold card after that. Then it's the top tier of our membership, the diamond card. As your membership is at the entry level, your baggage allowance depends on the ticket you buy. You will have extra baggage allowance when you become a silver member.

Y: I see. So now I am still an ordinary passenger?

R: Not exactly. You still have priority to check in and boarding.

Y: What about the Lounge?

R: I am sorry that lounge access is merely for silver or above.

Y: It seems there is a long way to go to the lounge.

R: No, it is not that far. Just travel more with us.

Y: Okay. Thank you. Sorry for bothering you.

R: No, not at all.

譯文

Y: 不好意思，因為我最近剛加入你們的飛行常客俱樂部，我有幾個關於會員的問題，我在想跟之前我加入的另一家航空的會員有沒有不同，以防我不小心跨了線（犯規）。

R: 當然！我很樂意。

Y: 謝謝你。我有點搞不清楚關於行李的上限。我到底可以帶多少？

R: 我懂。有時候這真是讓人困惑。我來解釋給您聽，楊先生。您剛加入我們的飛行常客，意思是說您現在是綠卡會員。當您的里程數累積到 30,000 哩，您就成為銀卡會員，再上去是金卡，再來是我們會員中最高等級的鑽石卡。因為您現在是剛加入階段，您的行李限額取決於您買的機票。您達到銀卡之後就會有額外的行李額度了。

Y: 我懂了。所以現在我只是個一般的乘客嗎？

R: 不完全是。您還是有優先辦理登機手續及優先登機的權利。

Y: 那貴賓室呢？

R: 很抱歉，貴賓室的使用要銀卡以上才可以。

Y: 看來到貴賓室還有很長一段路。

R: 不，沒有那麼遠。只要您多飛我們家的飛機。

Y: 好的。謝謝你。抱歉打擾你。

R: 不，一點也不。

英文母語者這麼說

I was wondering if there is any difference between this club and another airline club I joined earlier.（我在想跟之前我加入的另一家航空的會員有沒有不同。）

請注意「我在想」不要使用 I am thinking，因 wonder 是帶有「想要知道」、「感覺納悶」的意思，需要別人解答；而 think 則指「思考」、「認為」等，意思有點不一樣。在講英文時，請記得不要一味的將中文字面上一個字一個字翻成中文，有點像是當一個演員，不僅僅是字面上，還有「內心戲」要演、是有「情境」要考慮的！

字彙解析

- **membership** *n.* 會員身份
  It is free to join our membership.（加入我們的會員是免費的。）
- **frequent** *adj.* 經常的、頻繁的
  He is our frequent customer.（他是我們的常客。）
- **wonder** *v.* 納悶；想知道
  She is wondering where the ring is.（她正納悶戒指放哪去了。）
- **confuse** *v.* 困惑
  Her answer confuses me.（她的回答讓我好困惑。）
- **merely** *adv.* 只、僅僅
  It takes merely 1 minute from my house to the hospital.（從我家到醫院只要一分鐘。）

補充片語

❶ in case 萬一

例 The train is usually on time, but you'd better start early, just in case.（那火車通常是會準時，但你還是早點出門以防萬一。）

解 in case 也是常常會用到的片語之一，作為副詞使用。

❷ cross the line 跨過界線；犯規

例 He was punished as he crossed the line.（他因為犯規被懲罰了。）

解 以字面上的「超出界線」表示「犯規」。

❸ not exactly 不完全是

例 A: Do you mean she planned all these things? B: Not exactly.（A：你是說她策劃了這所有的事情？B：不完全是。）

解 exactly 表示肯定的回答；當想要回答「部份對、部份不對」的時候，可以使用 not exactly。

In Other Words

❶ Not at all. = No problem.（一點也不麻煩＝沒問題。）

解 兩句話雖然英文、中文翻譯起來都不一樣，但請記得講英文時，不是字面上一樣就好，請考慮整體情境。故文中要請對方「放心」、「不用客氣」的情境，可以用 No problem 表示「一點也不麻煩喔」。

地勤工作解說

通常會有兩種 VIP 櫃檯在機場裡：頭等／商務艙櫃檯及會員櫃檯。每家航空都有他們自己的飛行常客計畫，提供他們的常客在旅程中更多、更好的服務。「飛得越多，就有更棒的服務及回饋」。會員制度會將會員分成不同的階段，這些階段是由會員飛行累積的里程數或是飛行的「航段」來區分。加入會員並不是免費的，但是若你真的常常飛行，那麼這些服務及回饋都會比加入會員的入會費多，因此是很值得的。

前輩經驗巧巧說

航空公司為了留住常客，都會推出「會員制」的方式，讓這些重要客人固定只飛自己家的飛機。現在因為競爭激烈，就連廉價航空都開始有累積里程數或是點數的制度，來維持客人的消費忠誠度。會員也是有階級制度的（真的是個現實的社會）。飛得越多，哩程數越多，你的會員等級也越高。會員等級越高，可以帶更多的行李、可以進不一樣的貴賓室、可以多帶人進貴賓室、可以享有金色牌子的「行李優先領取」掛牌…等，都是航空公司祭出來吸引常客們「努力搭飛機」的方案，不為什麼，就是為了將大客戶留在自己家裡啊！而身為地勤人員，也要更用心、細心服務這些尊客，不然大客戶一個不高興，可是會選擇其他公司離去的唷！

1-5 行李托運

情境介紹

一位年輕男子於櫃台 check in，地勤人員為乘客辦理託運行李手續，並請客人等候行李通過安全檢查，而乘客於託運行李放置 3 個打火機，被安全人員攔下。

情境對話 Track 05

I ▸ Iris，Y ▸ Young Guy，S ▸ Security

I: Good evening, Sir. Your passport, please.

Y: Here you are.

I: Thank you. Let me see... You are flying to Kansai Airport directly. Any checked baggage?

Y: Yes. Just this one.

I: Please put it on the carousel.

Y: Okay. Is it overweight?

I: The baggage is just 20 kg. It isn't overweight.

Y: Great. I was worried that I have bought too many gifts.

I: That's great. Are there any restricted items inside?

Y: No.

I: Okay. Here are your baggage tag, please check, Taipei to Kansai. And this is your baggage reciept. Please put it away in case your baggage is lost. It will help us track your bag. May I have a look at your cabin baggage?

Y: Oh, here, only this one.

I: Thank you, Sir. Here are your passport and boarding pass. Have a nice flight. Please wait over there, until your baggage passes through the X-ray scanner.

Y: I see, thank you.(5 minutes later, at security)

S: Whose bag is this?

Y: Oh, it's mine!

S: Sorry, Sir. I saw something like lighters inside, would you please open it?

Y: Oh, yes, right, I bought them as presents. Is it restricted?

S: Sorry, Sir, you can only have one lighter without gas.

Y: What about the other two?

S: Sorry, you have to discard them. It is for the safety of the flight.

Y: Alright, I will leave them here.

譯文

I: 先生，晚上好。麻煩您的護照。

Y: 在這。

I: 謝謝。讓我看看…您今天直飛關西機場。

Y: 是。

I: 有需託運的行李嗎？

Y: 有，就這一個。

I: 請把它放到輸送帶上。

Y: 好的。有超重嗎？

I: 行李剛好 20 公斤，沒有超重。

Y: 太好了。我剛還在擔心我買太多禮物了。

I: 那真是太棒了。請問有任何禁止攜帶的物品在裡面嗎？

Y: 沒有。

I: 好的。這是您的行李掛牌，請您確認，從台北到關西（機場）。然後這是您的行李收據。請將它收好，萬一您的行李遺失了，它可協助我們將您的行李找回來。

Y: 我瞭解了。

I: 可以讓我看一下您的手提行李嗎？

Y: 喔，在這，就這一個。

I: 謝謝您，先生。這是您的護照及登機證。祝您飛行愉快。請您在那裡等候，直到您的行李通過 X 光掃描機。

Y: 好的，謝謝。（5 分鐘後，安全檢查處）

S: 這是誰的行李？

Y: 噢，是我的。

S: 抱歉，先生。我看到像是打火機的東西在裡面，可以請你打開它嗎？

Y: 噢，是，沒錯，我買了幾個要送人的，這樣不行嗎？

S: 抱歉，先生，你只能攜帶一個沒有瓦斯的打火機。

Y: 那另外兩個打火機怎麼辦？

S: 抱歉，為了飛航安全，你必須丟掉它們了。

Y: 好吧，我會把它們丟掉。

英文母語者這麼說

Please wait over there.

（請在那裡等候。）

不說 Please wait at there。there、here 這一類地方名詞的前面，通常不會加上 at 或 in，直接說 Please wait there 或 Please wait here，這樣的用法在文法上沒有錯，但若要更口語的用法，可以用 over there 表示「在那裡」、right here「在這裡」，有更加強調「那裡」、「這裡」的意味在。

字彙解析

- **directly** *adv.* 直接地

  Would you like to talk to your idol directly?（你想直接和你的偶像說話嗎？）

- **carousel** *n.* （行李）輸送帶

  Please keep away from the carousel, and please watch out for your children.（請不要靠近行李輸送帶，並請留意您的小孩。）

- **reciept** *n.* 收據
  Here are your change and receipt.（這是找給您的零錢與收據。）

- **X-ray scanner** *n.* X 光掃描機
  This X-ray scanner is under maintenance, please go to another path.（這台 X 光掃描機正在保養中，請走另一條走道。）

- **track** *v.* 追蹤，追溯
  I would like to track my luggage, but the computer system is unable to recognize my pronunciation.（我想追蹤我的行李，但電腦語音系統無法辨識出我的發音。）

補充片語

❶ have a look at 看一下

例 May I have a look at your bag inside?（我可以看一下妳包包裡面嗎？）

解 have a look（at）是「看一下」、「瞄一眼」的意思，也可以用 take 取代 have 變成 take a look（at），整體作一動詞片語使用。在機場因為有很多要檢查的項目，所以這個「看一下」、「瞄一眼」是常常會用到的詞，可以記下來靈活運用。

❷ I see. 我瞭解了。

例 A: Please take this sheet to collect your shoes. B: I see.（A：請拿這張單子來取回您的鞋。B：我瞭解了。）

解 I see 是非常常見的簡單片語，是「我瞭解了」或「我明白了」、「我懂了」，有時候作「原來如此」的解釋，表示千萬不要翻成「我看見」，會很糗！see 如果解釋為「看見」的時候，後面一定會有人事物，完整表述一個句子，不會單獨出現 I see 這樣不完整的句子，請千萬要記住。

In Other Words

❶ Please put it away in case your baggage was lost. It will help us to track your bag. = Please keep it properly in case your baggage was lost, it will help us to track your bag.（請將它收好，萬一您的行李遺失了，它可協助我們將您的行李找回來。）

解 put away 是「收好」的意思，另一個常用來說「保存」、「收好」、「存放」的單字是 keep，搭過高鐵的人應該對這句話很熟悉 Please keep your personal belonging with you, and mind the platform gap when arriving.中文即為「下車時，請記得您的隨身行李，並請留意月台間隙」。

❷ Whose bag is this? = Who owns this bag?（這是誰的行李？）

解 whose 是疑問代名詞，表示詢問「誰的」的意思。因為是問「誰的」，我們也可以從另一角度來看，問「是誰擁有這個行李」，即 Who owns this bag?，這兩種說法都蠻常見的。

地勤工作解說

「掛行李」是地勤人員第一件要學習的事情。行李掛牌（或稱行李條）要怎麼撕開、怎麼貼上，每家航空公司雖有不同，但整體來說大同小異。在整個託運行李的過程，先確認乘客的目的地，再看有無轉機，有轉機的話後段航班是本家或是外家航空？若為外家航空再確認是否有簽訂行李合約，能不能直接掛到目的地，有時也要看乘客前往的國家有無特別的行李規定。比如說在美國轉機，就算是轉至美國境內也一定要在第一站將行李取出做安全檢查再次託運。乘客通常不了解地勤人員在櫃台到底在忙些什麼，其實在那小櫃檯上要確認的事情可不少唷。

前輩經驗巧巧說

在進入航空業當地勤之前，出國的時候都看到地勤人員在各自的櫃檯忙東忙西，常常手邊打字打得很快，也不知道在輸入些什麼。真的從事這行業後才知道，原來有這麼多東西要在短短幾分鐘的 check in 時間內完成，真的不容易。其中關於「行李」的規定是一大難題。除了各家航空公司都有不同的行李規定之外，自己家的乘客飛往不同國家也有不同的行李限額。另外，因為販售的機票艙等不同，也會有不同的行李規則，更不用說還牽扯到乘客有會員、搭商務艙、與嬰兒同行…等不同情況了。還有，各個國家為了安全考量，對乘客的行李運輸也有不同的規範，每一項都要確實檢查，才可以印出那長長的行李條呢。這還沒完，還要確認乘客行李有無超重、有無違禁品、手提行李多大、裝了什麼、有沒有超重…一架飛機動輒上百人，這就是為什麼辦理登機要在起飛 2 小時前就開始的原因了！

1–6 接聽電話

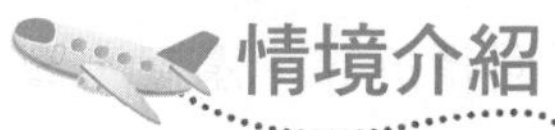

情境介紹

一位阿嬤要到美國看孫子，想帶一些中藥給女兒，幫她補身體，因為沒有自己出國過，打電話到機場詢問行李及一些去美國的相關問題。

情境對話 Track 06

A ▸ Allen，O ▸ Old Lady

(Ring ring)

A: Hello, Aloha Airlines. How can I help you?

O: Hello, I will go to America at the end of the month, and have some questions about packing up and the baggage. Would you help me?

A: Of course! What is bothering you?

O: My daughter who lives in L.A. gave birth to a boy yesterday, so I'm going to take care of her for a while. However, I am not sure if it is available to bring Chinese medicine with me. I am worried that they would confiscate the medicine.

A: About the Chinese medicine, many Chinese or Taiwanese get married in America in recent years, and many people bring Chinese medicine for their children. This situation is very common to the customs officers of America. Please feel free to bring it.

O: Oh, thank you. Another question is, how much can I have within my luggage?

A: May I have your ticket number? I think you can find it on your itinerary, which starts with 043.

O: Um... oh, it is 043 8989360000.

A: Okay, your baggage allowance is 2 pieces, 23kg each. It means you can have 2 pieces of luggage, which are 23kg and 23kg respectively. Additionally, you can have one cabin suitcase if you wish.

O: Are you saying that I can have my handbag and a cabin suitcase with me, and 2 pieces of large luggage for checking in?

A: Yes. As your carry-on baggage will be placed in the stowage overhead your seat, it needs to be under 7 kg for safety.

O: Okay. Thank you.

A: Thanks for calling, good day.

譯文

（電話響）

A: 您好，阿囉哈航空。有什麼需要服務？

O: 嗨，我這個月底要去美國，有些關於打包行李的問題，你可以幫我這個忙嗎？

A: 當然！什麼這麼困擾您呢？

O: 我住在L.A.的女兒昨天生了個小男孩，所以我要去照顧她一陣子。但是我不確定可不可以帶中藥過去？我怕他們會把藥沒收。

A: 關於中藥啊，因為這幾年很多中國人或台灣人在美國結婚，也很多人為了自己的孩子帶中藥過去的。這情況對美國海關相當常見。所以不用擔心。

O: 噢，謝謝你。噢，對了，有另一個問題是，我可以帶多少行李？

A: 可以給我您的機票號碼嗎？我想您可以在您的行程表上找到，它開頭是 043。

O: 嗯…噢，是 043 8989360000。

A: 好的，您的行李限額是兩件，每一件限制 23 公斤。意思是說您可以帶兩個行李箱，分別是 23 公斤、23 公斤。此外，若您想要的話，您還可以帶一個登機箱。

O: 你是說我可以帶我的手提包跟一個登機箱，和兩個托運的大行李箱嗎？

A: 是的。因為您的隨身行李會放置在頭上的置物櫃，所以必須少於 7 公斤才安全喔。

O: 好的。謝謝你。

A: 謝謝您打過來，日安。

英文母語者這麼說

My daughter who lives in L.A. gave birth to a boy yesterday, so I am going to take care of her for a while.（我住在 L.A. 的女兒昨天生了個男孩，所以我要去照顧她一陣子。）

在這裡要釐清 born 跟 birth 的差別。當我們說「我是 1988 年出生的」，英文會說 I was borned in 1988，born 是一個形容詞。而要把主詞變成生孩子的人時，就會用 give birth to，如 My sister gives birth to a baby，birth 是「誕生」為名詞，所以「生產」這個動作是用 give birth（to），可以想成「給了 baby 生命」的意思。

字彙解析

- **information** *n.* 訊息、資訊

  If you have any question, go to the information center.

  （你如果有什麼問題可以去資訊中心詢問。）

- **Chinese medicine** 中藥

  I have never tried any Chinese medicine because of the smell.

  （我從來沒試過任何一種中藥，因為它的味道。）

- **confiscate** *v.* 沒收

  The teacher confiscates their comic books.

  （那老師沒收了他們的漫畫書。）

- **customs officer** 海關官員

All customs officers have passed an exam.
（所有海關官員都通過了考試。）

- **stowage** *n.* 裝貨；放置物品處

The stowage is full, so I can't put my bag in.
（置物處滿了所以我無法放我的包包進去。）

補充片語

❶ at the end of 在…的最後

例 I am going to Taipei at the end of the month.（月底我要去台北。）

解 「at the end of ～」與「in the end」稍有不同。「at the end of ～」是指「在～的最後」，所以「at the end of the month」就是「月底」的意思，而「in the end」本身是一個副詞，就是「最後」的意思。

❷ pack up 打包

例 He is busy packing up.（他正忙著打包行李。）

解 pack 本身就有「打包行李」、「整裝」的意思在，而 pack up 也是常用片語，同樣是「整理行李」、「打包」的意思。

❸ take care of 照顧

例 Please take care of yourself.（請照顧好自己。）

解 take care of 後面加的是被照顧的對象。如果有朋友說他生病了，就可以請他 take care of yourself。

❹ for a while 一陣子

例 She has been sick for a while.（她已經病了好一陣子了。）

解 for a while 表示不太清楚多久，但已經有一段稍微長一點的時間。

In Other Words

❶ Of course! = Certainly!（當然！）

解 of course 是我們常用表示「當然」的句子，其實有另一個單字就可以代表 of course，那就是 certainly。certain 是「確定的」、「無疑的」、「可靠的」意思，certainly 就是副詞「當然」。

❷ I am not sure if it is available to bring Chinese medicine with me. = I am not sure whether Chinese medicine is available to bring with me.（我不確定是否可以帶中藥。）

解 whether 跟 if 一樣，都是「是否」的意思。而後半句則是將 it 這個替代整個事件（帶中藥）的詞省略，將 Chinese medicine 變成子句的主詞，整個子句就是 whether Chinese medicine is available to bring with me。

地勤工作解說

在機場，我們常常會接到不同的電話。若天氣不好，電話就接不完了，因為大家都想知道到底飛機會不會飛？平常則會接到詢問行李、飛機抵達時間、物品遺失在飛機上、行李還沒到、查詢訂位…各式各樣的電話都可能會接到，都要耐心回答。

前輩經驗巧巧說

一般來說，航空公司都會有很多支電話，其中一般旅客最常打的就是訂位組電話。但是因為訂位組有固定的上下班時間，不外乎上午 8 點半到下午 5 點半，跟一般上班族是一樣的。若要詢問有關票務的問題，其實打給訂位組會得到最多最正確的答案。但是一般乘客通常不了解，因此常會打電話到機場，覺得反正都是同一家公司，應該都知道。但航空公司分工很細，機場其實是處理現場的客人為主，並沒有特別安排人力接電話，都是在忙碌的工作之餘接的，所以若有票務問題，都還是會請客人打訂位組處理。

1-7 改名字

情境介紹

一位黃先生在機場，出發當天 check in 時，地勤人員無法找到他的訂位，與他核對電子機票，發現訂位時將名字漏了一個字母，地勤人員請他與旅行社聯絡，但找不到旅行社的人，只好現場於資訊櫃檯改，並支付 800 元。

情境對話 Track 07

A ▸ Agnes，H ▸ Mr. Huang，J ▸ Jill

A: Sorry, Sir. I can't find your booking record in the system. Do you have your itinerary with you?

H: Oh, yes. It is in my e-mail. Here.

A: Let me see. Oh, Sir. The name in the system is incorrect.

H: What?!

A: Here. The "A" is missing. That's why I cannot find your record.

H: Can't you just add it now?

A: I'm sorry I can't. Please contact your agent to correct it in the system.

H: Alright, I'll call him. But it's 6 in the morning! What if he didn't answer the phone?

A: We can correct it at the information counter, but you'll be charged, so I suggest we call the agent.

H: Charge for a letter!? For god's sake!

(20 minutes later)

H: (Sigh) I can't find him. Where can I correct it?

A: Sir. Please go to the information counter over there, thank you. (By walkie-talkie) Jill, there is a passenger. Mr. Huang, flying with XX451, has a wrong name in the system, please correct it for him. He's going to your counter now.

(A few seconds later)

J: Good morning, Sir. You must be Mr. Huang. Your passport and itinerary, please.

H: Here.

J: May I confirm with you that you're flying to Hong Kong this morning by XX451?

H: Right, right.

J: Please check your itinerary carefully next time. It charges $800 to correct the name at the airport, but free before you come here. Would you like to pay by cash or credit card?

H: By card! And I want a receipt! To ask for an indemnity from the travel agency!

J: No problem.

譯文

A: 抱歉，先生。我在系統裡找不到您的訂位紀錄。您有帶您的行程表嗎？

H: 噢，有。在我的 email 裡面。在這裡。

A: 我看一下。噢，先生。系統裡的名字錯了。

H: 什麼？！

A: 「A」不見了。這就是為什麼我找不到您的紀錄。

H: 你不能現在就把它加上去嗎？

A: 抱歉，沒辦法。請您跟您的旅行社人員聯絡，請他們在系統裡改。

H: 怎麼會？這從來沒發生過！

A: 我很遺憾。

H: 好吧，我會打給他。但現在早上 6 點耶！要是他沒接咧？

A: 我們可以在資訊櫃檯幫您改，但需要跟您收取費用，所以建議您打給旅行社。

H: 為了一個字母收費？！天哪！

A: 我很遺憾。

（20 分鐘後）

H: （嘆氣）我找不到他。我要去哪裡改？

A: 先生，請您到那邊的資訊櫃檯，謝謝。（透過無線電）Jill，有位乘客黃先生，搭乘 XX451，系統裡名字錯了，請幫他更正。他現在要過去你的櫃檯了。

（幾秒鐘後）

J: 早安，先生。您一定是黃先生吧？可以先給我您的護照和行程嗎？

H: 在這。

J: 先跟您確認您是搭乘今天早上 XX451 到香港嗎？

H: 對、對。

J: 請您下次仔細檢查行程表。在機場改名字要花 800 元，但來這之前都是免費的。您要付現還是刷卡？

H: 刷卡！還有我要收據！我要去跟旅行社要求賠償！

J: 沒問題。

英文母語者這麼說

Please contact your agent to correct it in the system.
（請與你的旅行社人員聯絡並於系統裡更正。）

小心不要說 Please contact with your agent to correct it in the system，因在此句中，contact 作為動詞，不用介系詞連接後面的名詞。

You must be Mr. Huang.（你一定是黃先生。）

請別說 You are Mr. Huang definitely，整句看起來的確是「你一定是黃先生」，但這個說法怪怪的。這裡的 must 是表示帶有自信的猜測，而 You are Mr. Huang definitely 像是在「定義」你是黃先生這件事。

字彙解析

- **record** *n.* 紀錄
  The record she held last year was broken yesterday.（她去年保持的紀錄昨天被破了。）

- **incorrect** *adj.* 不正確的
  The spelling of your name in the system is incorrect.（你的名字拼字在系統裡是不正確的。）

- **contact** *v.* 聯絡
  I suggest you contacting your lawyer.（我建議你聯絡你的律師。）

- **correct** *v.* 更正
  The data needs to be corrected, or we will lose the case.（那資料需要更正，不然我們會失去這個案子。）

- **agent** *n.* 代理人；代理商；仲介；這裡指的是旅行社負責的窗口
  You could call the agent to order the extra service.（你可以打給代理人訂購額外的服務。）

- **indemnity** *n.* 賠償
  The court made him pay an indemnity to his ex-wife.（法院判決他要賠償他的前妻。）

補充片語

❶ For god's sake! 天哪！看在上帝的份上，做個好事吧！

例 Let him go for god's sake!（看在上帝的份上就讓他走吧！）

解 用於加強請求的語氣或表示厭煩、驚奇等，常在帶有憤怒情緒時使用。

In Other Words

❶ The name in the system is incorrect. = The name in the system is wrongly typed.（系統裡的名字是不正確的。）

解 也可以說「系統裡的名字被打錯了」，wrongly typed 為「打錯了」，是被動式的說法。

❷ Please correct it for him. = Please redress it for him.（請幫他更正。）

解 re-開頭的字都帶有「再一次～」的意義在。redress 則是「糾正」、「更正」、「再次更新」的意思。

地勤工作解說

有時輸入名字卻找不到乘客的訂位紀錄，請確認是不是訂位在該航班，或是名字拼錯了、少了字母。旅行社在幫乘客訂位時，可能出現拼錯名字的狀況。然而對航空公司而言，名字拼錯可能就是換了一個人，因此在機場發現名字有錯誤的時候，若要現場更正，通常都會收取費用。

前輩經驗巧巧說

名字拼錯在機場還蠻常見的。通常處理的方式都是請客人打電話給旅行社，因為旅行社可以進入訂位系統更改，在飛行之前都還有機會更正，且這服務已經包含在當初他們向乘客收取的費用裡。但若遇到無法找到旅行社人員，或是由乘客自己透過網路訂位時就輸入錯誤，到機場才發現的話，那麼就只好在機場付費請現場人員協助更正。因此，在出發前一定要確認名字沒有錯，不然只好再多花錢了！

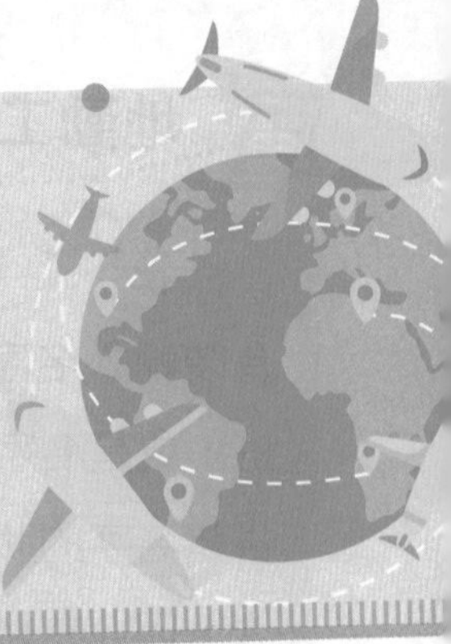

1–8 旅客臨時更改訂位

情境介紹

一位劉小姐從高雄飛香港轉機至北京，但由於高雄往香港飛機延誤，導致無法接上後段班機，在機場由地勤人員協助更改後段訂位。

情境對話 Track 08

A ▸ Allen，L ▸ Ms. Liu

L: I am going to Beijing via Hong Kong... which is... BC453.

A: I hope you will excuse me, Ms. Liu. Your flight, BC453, will be delayed for 1 and a half hours.

L: What? My flight to Beijing is only 1 hour later after I arrive in Hong Kong! How can it be possible to catch my ongoing flight?

A: Some part of the plane is out of order. For your safety, our engineers are fixing it up now. However, it takes time of necessity. I apologize for the inconvenience. The good news is that two sectors of your journey are both operated by our company, so we could rearrange your booking, and promise that you will be okay going to Beijing.

L: Really?

A: Yes, we have checked all possible flights from Hong Kong to Beijing that you could connect to, but it takes some time. Please wait a second.

(5 minutes later)

A: Thank you for waiting. Your new booking is completed. Here are your boarding passes of two sectors and luggage receipt, which is from Kaohsiung to Beijing. Our staff in Hong Kong will guide you to transfer.

L: Someone will guide me? How nice!

A: That is what we ought to do. I am terribly sorry to delay your trip, and thank you for your patience.

L: Well. It happens sometimes, not a big deal. Thanks!

譯文

L: 我要經香港轉機到北京…搭…BC453。

A: 我很抱歉，劉小姐。您的飛機 BC453 會延誤一個半小時。

L: 什麼？我去北京的飛機距離我抵達香港只有一個小時耶！這樣我怎麼可能搭上後段飛機？

A: 飛機某部分故障了。為了您的安全，我們的工程師正在搶修。但是需要花時間。造成您的不便我很抱歉。好消息是，您兩個航段都是由我們公司運行，所以我們可以重新為您安排訂位，並保證您可以順利到達北京。

L: 真的嗎？

A: 是的，我們已經查過所有從香港到北京可行的航班，讓您可以順利接駁，但這需要花一點時間。請您稍候。

（5 分鐘後）

A: 謝謝您耐心等候。您的新訂位已經完成。這是您兩段航程的登機證，然後這是您的行李收據，從高雄掛到北京。我們香港的工作人員會帶您去轉機。

L: 有人會帶我去嗎？真好！

A: 這是我們應該做的。對延誤您的行程我們感到很抱歉，並且感謝您的耐心。

L: 哎，有時候就是會這樣啦，沒什麼大不了。謝啦！

英文母語者這麼說

您的班機 BC453 將會延遲一個半小時。

中式英文：Your flight, BC453, will be delayed for 1 and half hours.

正確説法：Your flight, BC453, will be delayed for 1 and a half hours.

「一個半小時」的說法是 one and a half hour。英文中的「半小時」，前面要加上 a，很容易忘記，要特別留意。

字彙解析

- **half** *n.* 一半
  Half of this cake has been eaten when I found it in the fridge.（在我從冰箱裡發現這蛋糕的時候，它已經被吃掉一半了。）
- **possible** *adj.* 可能的
  Do you think it is possible that the Pyramid was built by aliences?（你覺得金字塔有沒有可能是外星人蓋的？）
- **engineer** *n.* 工程師
  My nephew wants to be an engineer when he grows up.（我姪子説長大後想當工程師。）
- **operate** *v.* 營運
  This plane was operated by our alliance airlines.（這架飛機是由與我們結盟的航空公司所營運。）
- **promise** *v.* 承諾
  He promised me that he will come back on Saturday.（他跟我承諾他星期六會回來。）

- **complete** *v.* 完成

  She completed her work and decided to go on a vacation.（她完成了她的工作並決定去渡個假。）

補充片語

❶ out of order 發生故障

例 My mobile phone is out of order.（我的手機壞了。）

❷ ought to 應該

例 I ought to know he was cheating on me.（我早該知道他在騙我。）

In Other Words

❶ I hope you will excuse me. = I am sorry. = My apologies. = I apologize. = You have my sincere apology. = Please accept my sincere apology. = I am awfully (or terribly) sorry.

解 這裏列出幾種表示「抱歉」、「對不起」的説法。其中最後一種 I am awfully sorry 中的副詞 awfully 也可用其他如 terribly 或 badly 替換，表示「非常抱歉」。

地勤工作解說

臨時更改訂位的情況有很多，這裡是因為乘客要在香港轉機，偏偏從高雄往香港的飛機故障，經工程部回報，修繕需要花一段時間，已經確定會延誤一個半小時，通常若前後段都是自己家的飛機，前段確定延誤且會耽誤後段行程，又是飛機故障這一類的因素，航空公司會負責協助更改客人的訂位，轉至可以銜接的航班，讓乘客順利抵達目的地。

前輩經驗巧巧說

飛機延誤的因素很多，最常見的就是天氣因素、機械故障及來機延誤，若非客人自己造成後段飛機接不上，又兩段航程皆為自己家的飛機，會極盡所能協助客人更改訂位，使之順利抵達目的地。筆者印象最深刻的一次是在夏天的雷雨季節，有一航班預計從香港飛往高雄後，同班飛機再載客回香港。來機沒有延誤，整架飛機順利辦理完登機手續，所有人都在登機門等候飛機抵達後，下客、整理機艙、再讓客人上機。沒想到就在飛機準備降落前 5 分鐘，機場一帶開始下大雷雨，機長看不見跑道，臨時決定轉降桃園機場！當時已經到了關櫃時間，也幾乎所有乘客都在候機室等候了，竟然在最後一刻得知飛機要延誤至少一小時，真的是一片嘩然！這一亂，除了要處理乘客的情緒，還要即時查詢有多少人要轉機、轉機到北京要接哪一班、到上海要接哪一班、還有沒有座位…那天就因為該班飛機，早班地勤從五點半上班到晚上七點半…（隔天許多人還是繼續早班五點半哪。）

1-9 現場購票

情境介紹

Amy 與家人因為高速公路大塞車而錯過了訂好的廉價航空班機，但因為是特惠機票不可改期或改搭乘其他航班，所以決定當場在機場其他航空公司的櫃檯重新購票。

情境對話 Track 09

K ‣ Ken，A ‣ Amy

A: Morning. My family and I missed our flight this morning at 7:30. I want to know whether you have any flight to Osaka today.

K: Yes, we have one flight to Osaka this afternoon at 2 o'clock and the estimated arriving time will be 5:40 pm.

A: Well, it's quite late, but is there any seat available on this flight?

K: Hold on a few seconds. I can double check the availability for you. (After checking the booking system) Yes, we still have a few seats available both on economy and business class now. Would you like to book this flight now?

A: Yes! We want to book three seats on economy class.

K: For your information first, if you buy the ticket here, it will be a full fare ticket and without any discount. Would you like to book one way or round trip ticket?

A: No problem. Round trip, please.

K: OK. Three economy class seats for the round trip. May I have your passports, please? Also, when do you plan to return?

A: Five days later. On January 26.

K: How would you like to pay? By credit card or cash?

A: Credit card, please.

K: (Finish the payment and booking)Ms. Chen, we would like to confirm the itinerary with you. Three economy class seats to Osaka on CX564 at 2 P.M. today and return flight will be CX565 at 11:30 A.M. on 26 January. If you'd like to change the date for the return flight, please contact our reservation office.

A: It's perfect. Thank you.

譯文

A: 早。我跟我家人錯過今天早上 7 點 30 分的班機，我想知道今天還有其他班機到大阪嗎？

K: 有的，今天下午 2 點有班機到大阪，預計抵達時間為下午 5 點 40 分。

A: 這麼晚啊，那這航班還有位子嗎？

K: 稍等一下，我幫您查詢是否還有機位。（查詢過後）今天往大阪的班機經濟艙及商務艙都還有機位。請問您是否有要訂位呢？

A: 好！幫我訂三個經濟艙的位子。

K: 不好意思，想告知您，如果在現場購票是全額票，無任何折扣。您今天想訂單程還是來回呢？

A: 沒問題。麻煩訂來回票。

K: 好，三張經濟艙的來回票。可以給我您們的護照嗎？還有，您們預計幾號回來呢？

A: 五天後，1 月 26 日。

K: 想要怎麼付款呢？用信用卡還是現金呢？

A: 信用卡。

K: （完成付款及訂位）陳小姐，跟您們核對一下行程。今天下午三位搭乘 CX564 下午 2 點的經濟艙到大阪，回程是 1 月 26 日早上 11 點 30 分 CX565。如果您想更改回程的時間，可以與我們訂位組聯繫。

A: 很好，謝謝。

英文母語者這麼說

Is there any seat available on this flight?

（這航班還有位子嗎？）

有時候我們會被中文誤導，詢問是否還有空位時，會不小心說成"Is there any empty seat on this flight?"，正確說法應如以上提出的例句，用 available 來詢問空位，或像是訂房詢問空房等等。

字彙解析

- **estimated arriving time** 預計抵達時間
  The estimated arriving time of this flight will be 5 P.M.（這航班預計會於下午五點鐘抵達。）

- **one way** 單程
  Kelly bought a one way ticket to London because she is not sure when the next semester ends.（因為凱莉不知道下學期什麼時候結束，所以只買了到倫敦的單程機票。）

- **round trip** 來回旅程
  You can buy a round trip ticket at a budget price.（你可以用划算的價格買一張來回票。）

- **available** *adj.* 可用的；可得到的
  Is there any available aisle seat near the emergency exit on this flight to Milan?（往米蘭的航班上還有逃生門附近的走道位嗎？）

- **payment** *n.* 支付；付款

  Full payment must be made before you issue the ticket.（開票之前必須要先完成付款。）

補充片語

❶ make a reservation 訂票；訂位

例 I would like to make the reservation for the flight to London on 31 December.（我想要訂一張 12 月 31 日飛往倫敦的機票。）

解 大多人都是在網路上或是跟台灣旅行社購買機票，這兩種方式都有可能出現先訂位後付款的情形，這時候的訂位就是使用 make a reservation，先預訂位子，付款之後確認行程與座位。除了使用在購買機票上，也可使用在一般餐廳訂位等等。若是不使用片語 make a reservation，也可單使用一個動詞 reserve 替代，可改成 I would like to reserve a business class seat on the flight to London on 31 December. 此外，也可以使用 book，但 reserve 較為正式。

❷ issue a ticket / ticket issuance 開票

例 If you do not pay before the deadline, your travel agency won't issue the ticket, and your reservation will be canceled.（如果您不在期限內付款，您的旅行社將不會開票，您的訂位也將被取消。）

解 購買機票時，有許多旅行社可以讓客人先訂位再付款，付款後隨即開票，開票的英文即為 issue a ticket 或是名詞 ticket issuance。一定要在完成開票後，才可真正確定機位；許多人會忘記或是延遲付款，機位就會在期限過後或是航空公司清票時被釋出。

In Other Words

❶ When do you plan to return?
=When would you like to return?
=When do you want to return?

解 這三句以第二句最有禮貌，would like to（=want）是服務業常用到的片語。對話中使用第一句則是因為不確定對方是否會因為去程時間較晚，進而不確定的回程時間，使用 plan 一詞給乘客有選擇的彈性。

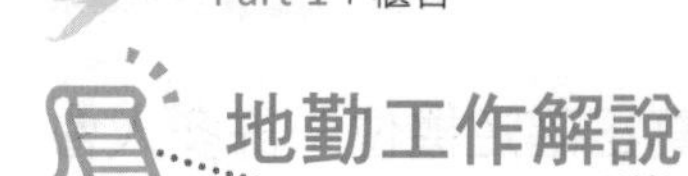

地勤工作解說

通常旅客很少會到機場才買票，會到機場買票的旅客大多分兩種，一種為晚到或是到現場才發現票無法使用的旅客，另一種則為完全沒有訂位的旅客；如遇到第一種旅客，可以先幫忙確認他的訂位及機票限制，如果可以更改就不用重新買票，限制較嚴謹的就必須現場購票。若是需要現場買票的旅客，我們會先確認他的目的地及來回程的時間，確認都還有位子可預訂後，跟旅客確認護照及簽證等資料，確認都沒問題之後就可以付款開票。除此之外，我們也會特別提醒旅客在機場買機票是全額票，價格會相當高，但機票幾乎完全無限制。

前輩經驗巧巧說

許多人買機票都是在網路上（像是官網或是購票網站）或是透過旅行社訂位，只有少數旅客會到機場現場買票。大部分的旅客都了解在機場現場購票的價格會偏高，但不知道怎麼區分或是大約多高，許多航空公司在現場賣的票價都是原價（全額票），完全無折扣，價格與網路上比通常是大相逕庭。

曾在櫃檯遇過因為忘記開票、兌換票忘記付稅金、記錯航班時間等等因各式原因得在票務櫃檯買票的旅客，通常前兩種如果時間不緊急，可以透過旅行社或是會員中心立即處理開票，只要還有訂位就可以解決。至於記錯航班時間或是錯過班機的旅客，如果機票的限制比較少，只要有空位就可以候補，但如果限制比較嚴謹的，像是只能搭指定日期的指定航班或是需加收其他費用的票就可能會需要現場買票。

如果在櫃檯遇見需要現場購票的旅客，我通常都會建議他們上網訂票或是找熟識的旅行社幫忙開票，因為價格會差相當多；像有一次有位乘客因為兌換票開票錯誤，決定現場買一張單程往香港的機票約台幣一萬六千多元，我建議他上官網看價格；他點選單程票，價格跟在現場購票差不多，於是我試著幫旅客買來回票（回程亂點選一天，但盡量在七日內），果然便宜許多，只需要約台幣六千多元。其實買票都會有一些秘訣，現場買一定比較貴，單程也會比來回貴；不常搭飛機的旅客都不會知道這些秘訣，地勤可以適時給他們協助，讓他們對公司留下好印象，也讓他們的旅程有個開心的開始或是結尾。

1-10 機位超賣

情境介紹

Brookes 先生持往曼谷的機票至機場櫃檯，發現機位超賣，已經劃位完畢，但 Brookes 先生堅持要當天前往，因此地勤人員將乘客轉往他航。

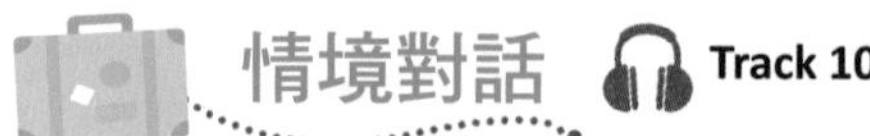

情境對話 Track 10

J ▸ Joanne，B ▸ Mr. Brookes，C ▸ Carol

J: I'm sorry, Sir. The flight to Bangkok is fully booked right now.

B: What? But I paid for the ticket already! What is the problem?

J: No, Sir. There is no problem with the ticket. It's just that the flight is overbooked today due to high season.

B: Why don't you just sell the exact number of tickets?

J: I'm sorry. It's the company's policy to reduce the cost for reasons that some people booking tickets won't take the flight.

B: I don't care. I paid for the ticket and have to go home today.

J: Okay, we can transfer you to another airline. We have a contract with Flora Airlines. If there is a seat, you can fly today.

Is that okay for you?

B: Okay. I prefer leaving here as soon as possible.

J: Please come with me.

(At the information counter)

J: (To her colleague) This passenger is going to Bangkok. Please give me FIM.

B: What is that?

J: This is FIM, the flight interrupt manifest. It's for the purpose of transferring our passengers to Flora or other airlines. It depends on passenger's destination and the time.

(At Flora Airlines counter)

J: Hello, Carol. This is Mr. Brookes. He needs to go to Bangkok. Is there any available seat for him? Here is his FIM.

C: Oh, you're really lucky. A customer just cancelled his ticket.

B: Does it mean I can go to Bangkok now?

J: Yes, Mr. Brookes, I apologize if any inconvenience caused.

譯文

J: 抱歉，先生。這班飛機已經滿了。

B: 什麼？但我的確付了機票錢啊！問題是什麼？

J: 不是，先生。您機票沒問題。是今天飛機座位超賣了，因為是旺季。

B: 你們為什麼不賣剛好的數量就好？

J: 我很抱歉。這是公司政策，有些人會訂位但不來搭機，這是為了降低成本。

B: 我不管，我付了機票錢而且今天就要回家！

J: 好的，先生。我們跟花花航空有簽約，可以將您轉到其他家航空，如果有位子，您今天可以飛。這樣可以嗎？

B: 好。我想要越早離開越好。

J: 那請跟我來。

（在資訊櫃檯）

J: （對她的同事）這位乘客要去曼谷，請給我 FIM。

B: 那是什麼？

J: 這是 FIM，放棄航班聲明，是用來將我們的客人轉到花花或其他航空用的，轉到哪一家是要看乘客的目的地跟時間而定。Brookes 先生，請跟我來。

（在花花航空櫃檯）

J: 哈囉，Carol。這是 Brookes 先生，要前往曼谷。你們還有位子給他嗎？這是他的 FIM。

C: 噢，你真的運氣很好。有個客人剛剛取消他的票。

B: 意思是說我可以去曼谷了？

J: 是的，現在沒問題了。Brookes 先生，若對您造成任何不便，還請您見諒。

英文母語者這麼說

There is no problem with the ticket.

（這張票沒有問題。）

通常說「～沒有問題」，注意介系詞不是 on、in，請用 with。

Please come with me.

（請跟我來。）

這裡想跟說明 then 這個字，這裏作「那麼」解釋。有時候 then 作「然後」解釋時，若同一句子前有一完整句子，請記得加上 and 來連結兩個句子。也就是說，then 本身不可以當連接詞使用。如本句是獨立的句子，then 就作「那麼」解釋，不會解釋為「然後」。

字彙解析

- **exactly** *adv.* 確實地

  He received the parcel exactly.（他確實收到包裹了。）

- **high season** 旺季

  The ticket during high season is always expensive.（旺季的票總是很貴。）

- **policy** *n.* 政策

  The policy changes so fast that many people were charged without notice.（政策變得太快導致很多人還不知道就被收費了。）

- **reduce** *v.* 減少

  The profit of this season reduces about 7%.（這一季的利潤少了大約 7%。）

- **occur** *v.* 發生

  Typhoons occur frequently in this area.（颱風常發生在這一帶。）

- **insist** *v.* 堅持

  She insisted that she had paid for it.（她堅持她已經付過錢了。）

- **prefer** *v.* 較喜歡、偏好

  I prefer the green one.（我比較喜歡綠的那一個。）

補充片語

❶ go abroad 出國

例 Will you go abroad this summer?（你今年夏天會出國嗎？）

解 abraod 是「在國外」的意思，為一副詞；加上一個 go 形成 go abroad 則是「出國」的意思。

❷ as soon as 一…就…

例 Let's leave here as soon as the rain stops.（等雨一停我們就離開這。）

解 as soon as 是「一…就…」的意思。文中 as soon as possible 是「一有機會或可能就走」，可翻成「越快越好」會比較順。

In Other Words

❶ A customer just cancelled his ticket. = There is a customer just cancelling his ticket.（有一個客人剛取消他的機票。）

解 there is 開頭通常都是「有一個…」的意思。這裡因後面還有完整的句子，因此可以省略 there is，直接以名詞作為開頭述說整句話。使用 there is 開頭則是帶有稍微強調的語氣。

❷ Does it mean I can go to Bangkok now? = Do you mean I can go to Bangkok now?（意思是說我可以去曼谷了嗎？）

解 這句話因說話者問的重點在釐清「我可以去曼谷了嗎？」，因此前面用 does it mean 或 do you mean 都可以。

地勤工作解說

在旺季的時候，各航空公司都有機位超賣的狀況，這是為了降低公司的成本。若每架飛機都訂剛剛好的座位數，有些乘客可能訂位了卻在飛行當天沒有出現在機場，那這些位子就空下來了，這樣就造成公司的損失。因此在販賣機票時，業務部門會預估一個數字是超過機位的，盡可能填滿所有的座位。但是在旺季時，就有可能出現人比座位多的情形，這時就要將乘客轉至其他航班或是其他航空公司。

前輩經驗巧巧說

「超賣」絕對是地勤人員的夢魘。通常超賣都是發生在旅遊旺季，少數是發生在更換機型，由大飛機換小飛機，但此狀況較少，沒有人會無緣無故臨時更換機位相差那麼多的飛機導致超賣。機位超賣還有分狀況。若只有經濟艙超賣，商務艙還有位置，就會將單獨旅行且看起來狀況比較 ok，如商務客人通常穿著比較體面，就可能得到升等到商務艙。這雖然現實，但因為商務艙都是重要的客人，因此考量商務艙客人的權益，要升等的人一定要稍微篩選。若遇到商務艙客滿經濟艙超賣，則可能將客人轉往上一班或下一班飛機，最不願意的就是轉往他航，因為這代表這一張票就要給其他公司賺一筆了。偶爾也有商務艙超賣，若該班飛機有頭等艙可以升等還好，有的飛機沒有頭等艙，只剩經濟艙還有座位，非常非常少的情形下，會請客人降等（也幾乎是等著被罵的意思，除非你遇到天使客人），但通常這機會非常少，情非得已，沒有人願意惹惱重要客人的。

1-11 候補機位

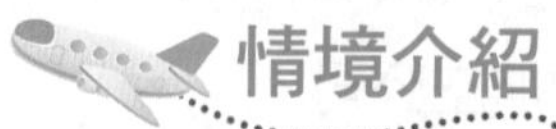

情境介紹

一位許先生持有台北飛往東京的機票，訂位紀錄中顯示他的訂位是在後天，但許先生希望能在今天飛過去，但因當日班機座位已經客滿，需要等待候補機位。

情境對話 Track 11

A ▸ Agnes，**H ▸ Mr. Hsu**，**S ▸ Sabrina**

H: Hi, I have this ticket from Taipei to Tokyo the day after tomorrow, but now I want to depart today. Is it available?

A: Let me check your booking record, please wait a moment... Um... yes, Mr. Hsu. You can change the date of flight without any charge. However, the flight to Tokyo today is fully booked. You need to wait for a while. Fill in the waiting list form at the information counter.

H: Okay, thank you.

(At information counter)

S: Hello. How can I help you?

H: I would like to go to Tokyo today, and this is my ticket.

S: Oh, okay. I will put you on the waiting list. Please fill in this form and wait here. We will let you know the result about 30 minutes later, which is the time to close counter.

H: Okay. Is there anybody else on the waiting list, too?

S: Um... yes. But don't worry. You are the first three passengers on the list, which means the chance to have a seat is comparatively high. Please remember to come back here 30 minutes later.

譯文

H: 嗨，我有一張票是後天從台北到東京，但我改變我的主意要今天去。可以嗎？

A: 讓我看看您的訂位紀錄…有，許先生。您可以變更您的飛行日期而且不用付費。但今天飛東京的班機訂位是滿的。您需要稍等一下喔。麻煩您到資訊櫃台填排候補的表格。

（在資訊櫃台）

S: 嗨，有什麼我能幫忙的嗎？

H: 我今天想去東京，這是我的機票。

S: 喔，好的。我會把您排在候補名單上。請您填一下這張表格，並且在這裡等候。我們大概 30 分鐘後會讓您知道結果，就是關櫃檯的那個時候。

H: 好的。有其他人也在候補名單上嗎？

S: 嗯，有。但不用擔心，您是名單上的前三位乘客，也就是說有座位的機會相對地高喔。請記得 30 分鐘後回到這裡來。

英文母語者這麼說

您是名單上的前三位乘客。

中式英文：You are the top three passengers on the list.

正確說法：You are the first three passengers on the list

the top three 是「前三名」，有名次的意味在裡面，請不要再混了。

字彙解析

- **available** *adj.* 有效的

  The ticket is not available as it is expired.（這張票是無效的，因為它過期了。）

- **fill** *v.* 填

  There are many forms to be filled before you enter the school.（進入這學校前有許多表格要填。）

- **form** *n.* 表格

  Please take this form to him and send it to me by email when he finishes it.（請將這表格交給他並請他完成後用 email 寄給我。）

- **comparatively** *adj.* 相對地

  The income of this city is comparatively high in the country.（這城市的收入在該國家裡相對地高。）

補充片語

❶ the first 前…位

例 The first three customers on our anniversary day will be awarded.（在我們週年慶那天的前三位客戶會頒獎給他們。）

In Other Words

❶ You can change the date of flight without any charge. = You are allowed to change the date of flight without any charge.

解 「你被允許更換飛行的日期」也可以說「你可以更換飛行的日期」，用 can 取代 be allowed。

地勤工作解說

有時候乘客會臨時想要更改飛行的日期，這都要取決於他／她的機票來決定是否需付費才能更改機票，有些機票甚至不能改日期（通常越便宜的機票彈性越小），要改日期得直接重買一張。文中乘客的機票是可以改日期的，但因為飛機訂位已滿，此時可以先幫客人辦理訂位，只是訂位狀態會跳「standby」，此時請客人先填寫候補的表格，等快要關櫃檯時，若有 no show 的乘客，飛機有空位，即可開始將 standby 的客人一一收進航班。

前輩經驗巧巧說

航班客滿的時候，各個櫃檯都會很忙碌。若有 standby 的客人，通常會請他們在 information 櫃檯附近的座位等候，並告知關櫃時間，屆時一定人要在場喔，通常客人都會說好好好，到了快關櫃檯時就會通知他們誰能搭上飛機。最麻煩的就是已經到了關櫃時間，要儘速將候補上的客人辦理登機，結果候補上的客人不知道跑到哪去了，又要花時間找人，真的很讓人崩潰。更崩潰的是，明明候補候上了，行李又超重、票又有什麼問題、解決之後要催客人快點跑不能逛免稅店…在機場真的像在打仗，非常的不輕鬆啊。

1-12 Late Show

一位先生飛往香港，但因路上塞車，已經過了關櫃時間才抵達。

H ▸ Mr. Huang，N ▸ Nancy，J ▸ Jill

H: Hi. I am taking JK457 to Hong Kong today. I know I'm late due to the traffic jam... anyway, can I catch the flight?

N: Oh, I'm sorry. The counter is closed. I think the boarding is almost finished.

H: Damn! Okay, then what can I do now?

N: Please come with me to the information counter. They will assist you to rearrange your trip.

(At information counter)

N: Jill, the passenger missed JK457, would you please help him?

J: No problem. Sir, may I have your passport and itinerary?

H: Here.

J: Okay... let me see... Mr. Huang, what we can do now is to transfer you to JK 455 which is still available today, and it will departure at 20:35. However, the ticket you hold shows that it charges $800 to do so. Is it okay to you?

H: So you mean it is not free?

J: According to the ticket policy, I'm sorry it's not.

H: Okay. Is there any earlier flight?

J: I'm afraid this is the earliest time of the flight we have today.

H: Uh...... alright!

J: Would you like to pay by cash or credit card?

H: By card, thank you.

J: Okay. This is your new itinerary and your passport. Please check in before 19:45.

譯文

H: 嗨。我原訂今天搭 JK457 去香港。我知道我遲到了因為塞車…總之，我還趕得上這飛機嗎？

N: 噢，我很抱歉。櫃檯已經關了。我想登機也差不多結束了。

H: 該死！好吧，那我現在該怎麼辦？

N: 請跟我到資訊櫃檯。他們會協助您重新安排您的行程。

H: 謝謝。

（在資訊櫃檯）

N: Jill，這位乘客錯過 JK457 了，你可以幫忙他嗎？

J: 沒問題。先生，可以給我您的護照及行程表嗎？

H: 這裡。

J: 好的…我看一下…黃先生，我們現在可以做的是，將您轉到 JK455，先在這班飛機還有位子，將於 20:35 起飛。但是您的票顯示這要收您 800 元。請問這樣可以嗎？

H: 所以你是說不是免費的？

J: 我很遺憾不是。這張票的規定是這麼寫的。

H: 好吧。那有其他更早的飛機嗎？

J: 恐怕這是今天時間最近的一班飛機了。

H: 呃…好吧！

J: 請問您要用現金支付還是刷卡？

H: 刷卡，謝謝。

J: 好的。這是您新的行程表及護照。請您於 19:45 前辦理登機。

英文母語者這麼說

（他們會協助您重新安排您的行程。）

中式英文：They will assist you to arrange your trip again.

正確說法：They will assist you to rearrange your trip.

「重新安排」可以使用 rearrange，因為 again 雖然有「再次」的意思，但 rearrange 有種「重新整理」的感覺，與單純的「再一次」有微妙的不同喔。

字彙解析

- **traffic jam**　交通阻塞、塞車

  The traffic jam this morning was due to a car accident.（今天早上大塞車是因為一場車禍。）

- **catch** *v.*　趕上、及時趕到

  I didn't catch the flight.（我沒有趕上飛機。）

- **policy** *n.*　政策

  Some of the policy of the company is not rational.（這公司有些政策並不合理。）

補充片語

❶ due to 由於

例 The flight was delay due to failure of machine.（班機延誤是因為機械故障。）

In Other Words

Is it okay to you?

= Are you okay with that?（請問這樣可以嗎？）

解 第一句是把it當作主詞，指某件事物；第二句則是以你you為主詞。

地勤工作解說

有時候乘客會遇到一些狀況，導致沒有辦法準時抵達櫃檯辦理登機，而錯過了原本訂位的班機。若該乘客抵達櫃台的時間距離關櫃檯時間沒有很久，督導會視當天班機的狀況，盡可能的讓乘客搭上飛機。但若已經關櫃一段時間，甚至飛機都起飛了乘客才到，或是當天太多狀況需處理而無法再收客人，那只好跟他們說聲抱歉了。此時，會請客人出示機票，看他所持有的機票是否彈性夠大，能夠免費將他轉至其他航班。如文中的黃先生就需要給付 800 元才能轉至其他航班。

前輩經驗巧巧說

一般來說，關櫃時間通常為登機時間前 40～50 分鐘，各機場規定有些微的不同。若乘客真的太晚抵達機場，因為登機前還有許多作業要進行，畢竟搭飛機不是搭高鐵，票買了、行李拎了就可以衝進車廂。飛機上的「人」跟「物品」（也就是行李）是分開處理的，且貨運的部分還要計算重量、平均分配，餐點的部份還要跟空廚確認、訂餐、請他們送上飛機…等，都要做到精準才可以起飛。當然也有部份客人，明明是自己錯過辦理登機時間，還覺得才差 10 分鐘、明明就還沒有飛…在櫃台吵鬧、拍桌大罵。遇到這種情形，若真的有需要，航空公司是可以請航警協助處理的。

1-13 Online Check In

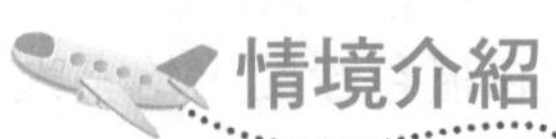

情境介紹

一位香港乘客要回港，使用 online check in，到機場託運行李，並印出登機證。

情境對話 Track 13

S ▸ Stacy，C ▸ Mr. Cheung

C: I have already checked in online . I just want to check in the baggage.

S: Okay. May I have your passport and the Taiwan Entry Permit?

C: But I have checked in online!

S: Yes, but we still need your passports to confirm your booking record and online check in record. Also, Taiwan Entry Permit is necessary, too. It is a part of our job ensuring you are ready to get on board.

C: I see. No wonder my agent told me not to put the entry permit into the check in luggage. Here you go. Can I check in my baggage now?

S: Yes, please. Besides, please refer to this statement, is there any restricted items in your luggage?

C: Is lithium battery restricted?

S: I'm afraid yes. Lithium batteries may be dangerous and can cause fire if improperly carried. Therefore, we always suggest our passengers to have it in hand carried bags.

C: Oh, then I have to take it out.

S: Have you printed out the boarding pass?

C: Not yet.

S: Okay... thank you. Just a moment, please.

C: Sure.

S: Here are the baggage receipt and boarding pass. Please wait for security check over there. Have a nice trip.

譯文

C: 我已經在線上辦理登機了，只是要托運行李。

S: 可以給我您的護照嗎？噢，還有入台證。

C: 但我已經線上登機了耶！

S: 是的，但我們還是需要您的護照以確認兩位的訂位紀錄及辦理登機手續的紀錄。另外，入台證也是必須的。確保兩位能順利登機也是我們工作的一部分。

C: 我懂了。難怪旅行社的人叫我別把入台証放在託運行李。在這，拿去吧。

S: 謝謝。

C: 我可以託運行李了嗎？

S: 是的，麻煩你。此外，請參考這張説明，有任何違禁品在您的行李裡嗎？

C: 鋰電池不能託運啊？

S: 恐怕是。鋰電池存放不當可能引起火災並產生危險。因此，我們都會建議乘客將它放在手提行李。

C: 噢，那我得把它拿出來。

S: 請問您有將登機證列印出來了嗎？

C: 還沒。

S: 好的…謝謝。請稍候。

C: 好。

S: 這是您的行李收據及登機證。請在那邊等候行李檢查。祝您旅途愉快。

英文母語者這麼說

Besides, please refer to this statement, is there any restrict items in your luggage?

（此外，請參考這張說明，有任何違禁品在您的行李裡嗎？）

這裏請注意不可以用 except 來表示「此外」。except 與 besides 的差別在於，besides 包含了前面所述的事物本身，但 except 是「除…外」，並不包含前面的事物，要特別小心使用。

We always suggest our passengers to have it in hand carried bags.

（我們都會建議乘客將它放在手提行李。）

「建議」這個字，英文裡常見的有 suggest 及 advice 兩個，在這裡我們會使用 suggest 而不用 advice，因為 advice 帶有「忠告」或是「勸告」的意味在，對客人當然是要柔和一點，所以不會使用 advice 喔。

字彙解析

- **online** *adj.* 線上的

  You can buy it from our online shop and pay by credit card.（你可以在我們線上商店購買並用信用卡付款。）

- **Taiwan Entry Permit** 入台證

  She lost her Taiwan Entry Permit.（她把入台證弄丟了。）

- **ensure** *v.* 保證、確保

  Please ensure your being on time.（請保證你會準時。）

- **lithium batteries** *n.* 鋰電池

  Lithium batteries is not allowed in check in baggage.（鋰電池不能放託運行李。）

- **cause** *v.* 導致、引起

  Smoking may cause cancer.（抽菸可能導致癌症。）

- **therefore** *adv.* 因此

  She got a flu, and therefore couldn't come to school.（她感冒了因此不能來學校。）

- **print out** 列印

  Remember to print out your booking record.（記得把你的訂位記錄印出來。）

補充片語

❶ get on board 上（交通工具）

例 It is time to get on board.（該是上車的時候了。）

❷ no wonder 難怪、怪不得

例 No wonder you can't sleep as you drank 2 cups of coffee.
（你喝了兩杯咖啡難怪睡不著。）

In Other Words

❶ No wonder my agent told me not to put the entry permit into the check in luggage. = So that's why my agent told me not to put the entry permit into the check in luggage.（怪不得我代理人叫我不要把入台證放在托運行李。

解 no wonder 是「難怪」、「怪不得」的意思，因此在這裡也可以說 so that's why 也是「怪不得」的意思。

❷ Besides, please refer to this statement, is there any restrict items in your luggage? = In addition, please refer to this statement, is there any restrict items in your luggage? = Additionally, please refer to this statement, is there any restrict items in your luggage?（此外，請參考這張說明，有任何違禁品在您的行李裡嗎？）

解 這裏要替換的詞是 besides，表示「除此之外」，可以用 in addition 或是 additionally 來代替。

地勤工作解說

幾乎每家航空都有線上辦理登機作業的服務。乘客可以在飛行前 48 小時自行在網上辦理登機，且有些乘客可能會自行將登機證列印出來。然而，若這些乘客有要托運的行李，還是需要到櫃檯辦理。此外，即使他們沒有要托運的行李，地勤人員還是需要確認乘客的簽證，以防乘客被遣返。若他們沒有到櫃檯來報到，地勤人員可能會在登機門廣播找尋乘客。這事關出入境，所以所有的步驟都要做到，沒有例外。

前輩經驗巧巧說

讓乘客線上辦理登機作業方便大家搭飛機，省去了在櫃檯辦理 check in 的時間。但如果有行李要托運，乘客還是得到櫃檯排隊，現在有些航空公司開了優先讓已於線上辦理登機的乘客專用託運行李的櫃檯，亦讓乘客省了不少時間。但要特別留意的是，乘客是否已經持有前往國家的入境許可，如簽證、有效的護照等，以免客人抵達後不能入境被遣返。若乘客在線上辦理登機且印出登機證，又沒有要托運的行李，可能就不會到航空公司櫃檯報到，此時，為了確保每位乘客順利抵達、入境，我們會在登機門廣播，或是在系統裡註記，當要登機過登機證時，機器會提醒這些有註記的乘客，就可以在登機門將這些客人攔下來檢查了。

1-14 樂器托運

情境介紹

旅客 Kevin 帶著一把吉他到櫃台劃位，旅客想將吉他拿上飛機。

情境對話 Track 14

L ▸ Lily，K ▸ Kevin

L: Good afternoon, Sir. How much baggage would you like to check-in?

K: Only one baggage.

L: Sir, how about the guitar you carry? Would you like to check-in it?

K: No! I will carry this guitar to the cabin.

L: I'm sorry to inform you that the guitar is not allowed in on board.

K: Why not? I'm afraid that the guitar will be damaged as in check-in bag. It's fragile item.

L: I understand your concern; however, a sturdy and protective hard case used for music instrument weight 5kg and its size is

78cm x 25cm x 15cm so that it can be easily carried to the cabin and safely settled in the cabin storage room. Please understand the rule. It is for all passengers' safety.

K: I see. Is there any way to avoid this guitar being damaged as check-in bag?

L: I will tag this guitar here and you can take it by yourself to the boarding gate then hand in it to our ground staff. Your guitar won't be harmed through the carousel at counter.

K: Thanks for your suggestion. Here is my guitar.

L: Ok, I will put one bag tag and a shipside offload tag on your guitar and also remind our staff to handle it with care.

譯文

L: 午安，先生。請問您有幾件行李需要托運？

K: 只有一件。

L: 那您攜帶的那把吉他呢？您要將它拖運嗎？

K: 不！我要帶這把吉他進機艙。

L: 很抱歉必須告訴您，這把吉他無法被帶上飛機。

K: 為何不可以？我怕我吉他托運會受損因為它是容易損壞的物品。

L: 我瞭解您的顧慮，然而，手提樂器和外面的保護硬箱尺寸限制是 **78x25x15** 公分，重量是五公斤，這是為了方便攜帶至客艙，且可以安全地放在機倉儲物櫃中。請您體諒這項規定是為了機上所有旅客的安全。

K: 我明白了。那有什麼方法可以避免吉他當成托運行李時受損嗎？

L: 我會先在這裡將吉他掛上牌子，然後讓您自行拿著吉他去登機門，再轉交給我們地勤。您的吉他就可以不會因為經過櫃台的運輸帶而受損。

K: 謝謝你的建議。這是我吉他。

L: 好的，我將會掛上行李條和機邊卸載的掛牌，也會提醒我們工作人員小心搬運您的吉他。

英文母語者這麼說

請問你有幾件行李需要托運？

中式英文：**Do you have how much bags to check-in?**

正確句子：**How much baggage would you like to check-in?**

Do you have 口氣上較為直接且不禮貌，不建議使用。

字彙解析

- **allow** *v.* 允許
  Riding a motorcycle is not allowed in this park.（在公園禁止騎摩托車。）

- **damage** *v.* 損壞
  This building was badly damaged by the earthquake.（這棟大樓在這次地震中受到嚴重的損壞。）

- **fragile** *adj.* 易碎的；脆弱的
  Be careful to move this box. There are a lot of fragile items inside it.（請小心搬運這個箱子，它裡面有很多易碎物品。）

- **sturdy** *adj.* 堅固的
  The table is made by sturdy material.（這張桌子是由堅固的材質而做成的。）

- **protective** *adj.* 保護性的；防護的
  Please wear protective mask and goggles when doing experiment.（做實驗時請戴防護面具和眼罩。）

補充片語

❶ carry sth. on board 帶……上飛機／登船

例 **Jason will carry one small luggage on board (this flight).**（傑森會帶一件小的行李上飛機。）

解 攜帶某物搭乘交通工具，接 **on board** 後即可省略交通工具一詞。

❷ hand in 提交；交給；遞交

例 **Please hand in the essay to professors before this week.**（請在這星期前提交論文給教授。）

解 將某物交給某人可用 **hand in** 片語來強調是由本人親自交出去的。

❸ handle sth. with care 小心處理；小心搬運

例 **Please mark wording, "handle with care" on the outer packing.**（請在這箱子的外包裝註明「小心搬運」。）

In Other Words

❶ The size of music instrument carried as cabin is 78cm x 25cm x 15cm and the weight is 5kg. = Carry-on music instrument within the size of 78 cm x 25 cm x 15 cm and within the weight of 5 kg.

解 「手提上機」航空英語常用 carry-on 來表達，例如 carry-on baggage，因此可用 carry-on 來代替句子 carry sth. as cabin。另外，within 有不超過的意思，可用來強調在尺寸規訂在特定的範圍內。

❷ I will put one bag tag and a shipside offload tag on your guitar. =Your guitar will be sticked on one bag tag and shipside offload bag tag.

解 此句可用被動式表達來強調吉他為主角。stick on 是黏貼的意思，因為行李條都是有背膠的，因此動詞可以 stick on。

地勤工作解說

基於飛航安全考量，避免旅客如遇上不穩定氣流晃動而導致座位上方儲物空間內的手提行李掉落砸傷乘客，因此航空公司規定每位旅客可攜帶一件手提行李的尺寸不能超過 56x36x23 公分和重量 5 公斤。不過針對可攜帶上飛機的樂器，尺寸有特別規定 78 公分 x25 公分 x15 公分。且不管樂器要手提或托運，都必須把樂器存放於堅固且具有保護作用的硬樂器箱內。如樂器存放於軟樂器箱內，樂器將不能接受作手提或托運行李處理。

前輩經驗巧巧說

一般旅客會認為因樂器屬於貴重且易損壞的物品，而不想將樂器托運，擔心會因為行李運輸帶受到撞擊。但又礙於手提上機的樂器有尺寸限制，因此常常在劃位櫃檯碰到旅客拒絕將樂器托運的情況發生，此時，地勤人員必須耐心地向旅客解釋並站在旅客角度為出發點，提出多種建議來減低旅客的擔憂。航空公司會提供「小心輕放」的警示標籤來提醒搬運人員。此篇對話中，地勤還提供另一種方法，讓旅客自行攜帶樂器至登機門再交由工作人員將它放置貨艙，這樣一來，可以避免樂器經過櫃台運輸帶的碰撞而受損，旅客或許會因為地勤人員提供的多種的保護方式而放心將樂器托運。

1-15 Cabin Bulky Baggage(CBBG) 佔位手提行李

情境介紹

旅客 Louis 攜帶大提琴從高雄前往米蘭，因為不想將大提琴託運，而決定幫大提琴購買機位，並已聯絡訂位組訂妥此項特殊需求。旅客攜帶大提琴前來機場劃位櫃檯。

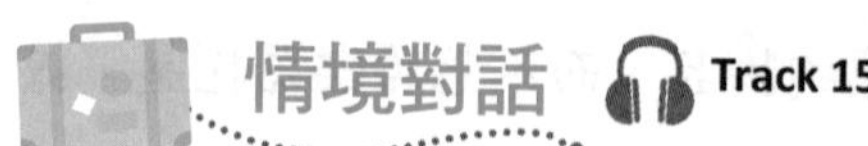

情境對話 Track 15

J ▸ Joanna，L ▸ Louis

J: Sir. I check your reservation record; there's going to be an extra seat for your cello.

L: That's right, and I have already put my cello into the hard case.

J: Ok, we will arrange one window seat for your cello and you will sit next to it. Is there any bag to be checked-in?

L: Yes, I would like to check-in this suitcase.

J: Ok, here is the boarding pass and bag receipt for you. As you can see, 37B is for you and 37A is for your cello that are showed on this boarding pass. Please be advised that you need to arrive at the boarding gate 40 minutes prior to the scheduled departure time for your cello handling procedure.

L: Can I ask that how my cello will be installed?

J: Our staff will use a canvas bag to secure the musical instrument to the seat then tie-down your cello on passenger seat. One more thing remind you that the strings have loosened to avoid damage due to temperature variations, expansion and contraction of the neck of stringed instruments may occur.

L: Ok, I understand. Thanks for your reminder.

譯文

J: 先生。我查看您的訂位記錄，您有幫您的大提琴多購買了一個位子。

L: 沒錯。我也把大提琴裝在硬箱子裡了。

J: 好的，我們將安排一個座位給您的大提琴，而您就坐在大提琴旁邊。有其他的行李要託運嗎？

L: 有的，我想將這個行李箱託運。

J: 好的，這是您的登機證和行李收據。就如同您看到的，登機證上秀的 37B 是您的位置，而 37A 是您大提琴的位置。請留意您必須在航班表訂的起飛時間前 40 分鐘到達登機門以便您的大提琴安裝程序。

L: 請問您們如何安裝我的大提琴呢？

J: 我們的工作人員將會使用一個帆布袋套在樂器外，並固定您的大提琴在乘客座位上。另一件事須提醒您，由於氣溫的變化，弦樂器的琴頸可能發生膨脹或收縮，建議您把琴弦放鬆以避免損壞。

L: 好的，我明白了。謝謝您的提醒。

英文母語者這麼說

（請留意您必須在航班表訂的起飛時間前 40 分鐘到達登機門，以便您的大提琴安裝程序。）

中式英文：**Please advise that you have to arrive the boarding gate before 40 minutes of departure time for handling your cello.**

正確說法：**Please be advised that you need to arrive the boarding gate 40 minutes prior to the scheduled departure time for your cello handling procedure.**

中文說「請留意」大部份人會直接翻譯為 *Please advise* 忘記用被動式用語，因為這句話是對旅客說，旅客為被告知的人，應用 *Please be advised*，如按照中式英文的文法會變成地勤人員請求旅客告知事情，句意傳達完全相反。另外，「*before 40 minutes of departure time*」雖然文法上看似沒錯，但應該將 *40* 分鐘放在 *before* 前面，且可以用 *prior to* 來替代 *before* 較為正式的說法。

字彙解析

- **cello** *n.* 大提琴

  Annie likes to play a cello in her leisure time.（Annie 喜歡在空暇時拉大提琴。）

- **procedure** *n.* 程序；步驟

  If you follow the standard procedure to use this machine, this machine won't be out of order.（如果你有按照標準程序使用這台機器，這機器不會壞掉。）

- **install** *v.* 安裝

  The air conditioner will be installed next week in the living room.（下週將會在客廳安裝冷氣。）

- **canvas** *n.* 帆布

  The material of this bag is canvas.（這包包的材質是帆布。）

- **string** *n.* 弦；細繩

  Stacy adjusted the strings on her violin before the performance.（Stacy 在演出前調過小提琴上的弦。）

- **loosen** *v.* 鬆開

  Please do not loosen your seatbelt when the airplane takes off.（飛機起飛時請不要鬆開你的安全帶。）

- **variation** *n.* 變化

  The variation of temperature is unusual recently.（最近氣溫的變化不太正常。）

補充片語

❶ prior to 在…之前

例 **Passengers are able to do an internet check-in 48 hours prior to departure time.**（旅客們可以在航班起飛前 48 小時前上網劃位。）

❷ tie-down 拴住；綁住

例 **The surfboard is tied-down on the car roof.**（這個衝浪板被綁在車頂上。）

In Other Words

❶ Please be advised that you need to arrive at the boarding gate 40 minutes prior to the scheduled departure time for your cello handling procedure. = Please be showed up at least 40 minutes previous to the departure time to allow time for us to install your cello.（請留意您必須在航班表訂的起飛時間前 40 分鐘到達登機門以便您的大提琴安裝程序。）

解 「show up 出現」please be showed up 就是請旅客出現在登機門可簡化原文中的 please be advised that you need to arrive。「prior to 在…之前」也可用另外的片語「revious to～替換，然而替換句子中的「allow time 有時間』可指出為何要求客人必須在起飛前 40 分鐘到登機門，因為需要有充足的時間固定樂器在位置上。handling procedure 其實就是說安裝樂器在位置上，因此也可直接用 install your cello。

❷ Our staff will use a canvas bag to secure the musical instrument to the seat then tie-down your cello on passenger seat. = The musical instrument will be packed with a canvas bag to secure and tied-down on passenger seat.（我們的工作人員將會使用一個帆布袋套在樂器外並固定您的大提琴在乘客座位上。）

解 換句話說的句型將主詞變為成樂器，因此就需要用被動式來表達樂器被包裝。pack with 用某物來包裝。替換句子內的動詞必須都是被動式。

地勤工作解說

旅客如有貴重物品不想因為託運而受損，航空公司針對此項提供了特殊服務，旅客可幫物品購買機位而攜帶上飛機，稱之「佔位手提行李 Cabin Bulky Baggage」，簡稱為 CBBG。然而因航空安全考量，並非所有物品都能是佔位行李，例如比較常見的物品為宗教佛像、樂器、藝術品、骨灰甕等。旅客必須於出發日期前三天撥打至當地訂位組要求此項服務，但物品尺寸須符合航空公司的規定才能被受理。

前輩經驗巧巧說

地勤人員幫旅客與 CBBG 劃位時，務必安排物品於窗戶位，因為這樣可使得佔位行李有所倚靠而避免物品因晃動而滑落於走道。由於安裝佔位行李需要較長的時間，因此在辦理好劃位後，一定要告知旅客在班機起飛前 40 分鐘到達登機門，以免耽誤到其他旅客的登機時間。且物品必須要有堅固的外包裝，以防止在綑綁過程中破壞到物品本身。如有宗教佛像為佔位行李，工作人員在包裝過程中得盡量避免將神像放在地板，須將佛像放置在以椅子上安裝以示尊重，也要詢問旅客本身需幫佛像準備餐點嗎？安裝佔位行李的這些細節都必須留意。安裝於位置上時地勤人員會運用多條特殊的安全帶來固定住物品。

1-16 團體客人

情境介紹

一位領隊 Leo 帶領 30 人團體要經香港前往杜拜，其中一人的護照資料不完整，需請領隊先將該名團員護照資料補上，才能印出登機證。

情境對話 Track 16

J ▸ Joanna，L ▸ Leo，M ▸ Mr. Li

L: Hi, I have 30 members in total, but still 2 of them have not been here, is that ok?

J: Yes, I can check them in later. Please gather other group members at counter number 8. But first, please provide me Mr. Lin Cheng-Hui's passport because his passport information was not complete in the system.

L: Oh, right, he is the only one who did not hand in the passport when booking the tickets. Here, I have already collected it.

J: Thank you. Where is he now? I just check him in first.

L: (yell) Mr. Lin! Please bring your baggage here! You are the first one to check in!

M: Hi, here is my bag.

J: Okay, please leave it there. Oh, Mr. Li, I have to remind you that your baggage is already 25kg, I suggest you take something out.

M: Can't you share the weight to other group members?

J: Yes, I will, but to protect our staffs carrying the baggage, the limitation for one baggage is 23kg.

M: I see.

(20 minutes later, all members have checked in)

J: Sir, are the last two members here?

L: No... I called them but no one answered.

J: The counter will be closed in 5 minutes. Please keep on finding them.

L: Oh! There they are! Hey! (waving)

J: Great, then the flight can be on time.

譯文

L: 嗨，我總共有 30 個團員，但有兩位還沒到，這樣可以嗎？

J: 可以，我可以之後再幫他們辦登機。請其他團員在八號櫃台集合。但首先，麻煩先給我林成輝先生的護照，因為電腦系統裡他的護照資料不完整。

L: 喔，好，他是唯一一個訂票時沒有繳交護照的。這裡，我已經先跟他拿了。

J: 謝謝。他現在人在哪裡？我就先幫他辦理登機。

L：（大喊）林先生！麻煩帶著您的行李來這邊！您第一個辦登機！

M: 嗨，這是我的行李。

J: 好的，請將它放在那不要動…喔，李先生，我必須提醒您您的行李已經達到 25 公斤重了，建議您拿一點點東西出來。

M: 你不能幫我把重量分給其他團員嗎？

J: 會，我會，但單件行李重量上限是 23 公斤，這規定是為了保護搬運行李的工作人員。

M: 我瞭解了。

（20 分鐘後，所有團員都完整登機手續）

J: 先生，請問最後兩位團員到了嗎？

L: 還沒…我已經打電話給他們了，但沒有人接。

J: 櫃檯在 5 分鐘之內就要關閉了，請繼續找尋他們。

L: 喔！他們來了！嘿！（揮手）

J: 太好了，這樣飛機可以準時了。

英文母語者這麼說

Pease leave it there.（請將它放在那不要動。）

提到「放」、「放置」，很多人會直覺的想到 put 這個字。Please put it there 也沒有錯，「請把它放在那」，在此情境中，因地勤 Joanna 要測量客人的行李重量，所以希望客人將行李放著之後別再碰它，以免秤重有錯誤，所以使用 please leave it there 來強調「不要碰」這件事。

I suggest you take something out.（我建議您拿一點點東西出來。）

有些人喜歡使用 advise 來表示「建議」，的確 advise 也有「建議」的意思，但當說話方使用 advise 時，表示說話者自認為較有知識，帶有點指導的意味在。suggest 則是一般性的建議或是提出主意，比較有「你那樣 ok，我這樣也可以」，說話方不會讓人有高人一等的感覺，因此若在機場對客人提出「建議」的時候，用 suggest 會比較妥當。

字彙解析

- **gather** *v.* 集合；將…聚集

Please gather at the counter at 5 o'clock.（請在五點的時候在櫃檯集合。）

- **provide** *v.* 提供

He provided me some useful information of traveling to Netherland.（他提供給我一些有用的荷蘭旅遊的資訊。）

- **complete** *adj.* 完整的、全部的

The jigsaw is not complete because one piece is missing.（那拼圖不完整，因為有一片不見了。）

- **suggest** *v.* 建議

He suggested me to read this book.（他建議我讀這本書。）

補充片語

❶ leave... there 將～放在那（不要動它）

例 I ask him to leave his ipad there before he finish his homework.（我要他在功課寫完之前將他的 iPad 放在那不准動。）

解 這是一個常使用的說法 leave something there，即為「把它放在那，而且不要碰它」。leave 本身有「離開」的意思，leave something there 就是要你「離開那東西，讓他在那」，這樣去理解，會更容易喔。

❷ on time 準時

例 Our mission is to make the flight on time.（我們的任務是讓飛機準點。）

解 讓飛機「準點」是地勤的最終目的，這個片語非常常見，作一形容詞使用，放在要形容的人事物後面。另一個「準時」的說法是「on schedule」，「schedule」是「時間表」的意思，表示「按照時間表」。請不要翻成「在時間表上」（on the schedule 才是在時間表上，多了「the」）。

In Other Words

❶ Please gather other group members at counter number 8. = Please lead other group members meet at counter number 8.（請他們在八號櫃台集合。）

解 在情境中，是地勤 Joanna 請領隊 Leo 帶領他的團員們在 8 號櫃檯集合，因此使用 gather 是作「將…聚集」的用法。若要換句話説，可以説 Please lead the meet at counter number 8.因為 Leo 是領隊，所以請他 lead（帶領）團員們在 8 號櫃檯 meet（會合）。

地勤工作解說

剛上櫃檯時，第一個坐的櫃檯就是「團體櫃檯」。許多航空公司都會專門設立一個櫃檯供團體客人使用，以免佔用其他散客（個別飛行的客人）太多時間。因為一整團人都是前往相同的地方，過程也較為單純，公司就是藉由團體客人讓新進員工熟悉 check in 流程。

前輩經驗巧巧說

現在團體客人大多是經由旅行社訂位，因此在訂位時便會要求旅行社人員將團員們的護照資料輸入電腦訂位系統，就像一般旅客若自己在航空公司網頁訂票，都會需要填入一些如生日、國籍等資訊。

另外，雖然是旅行社帶團，有時候還是會遇到團員前往需簽證國家，卻沒有簽證的問題，有時候是因為該國簽證規定有變動，或是特殊身份（在臺灣可能會遇到中國及配偶要出國）需另外申辦文件的狀況。以前還會有役男要出國必須經過許可蓋章的手續，出國前沒有辦妥，當天就只能看著家人出國自己默默回家了。（之後若無所謂的「役男」，可能這種光景就不會發生就是了。）

1–17 旅客臨時變更行程

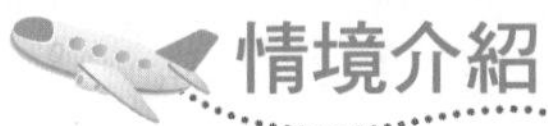

情境介紹

一位有澳洲護照的張先生，因媽媽病危要趕回 Brisbane。張先生持有一張後天由高雄至香港轉布里斯本的經濟艙 S 艙機票到機場，直接到 information 櫃台表示要趕回家。最後由訂位組協助訂好 Y 艙機票刷卡補差額，客人順利在當天飛回布里斯本。

情境對話 Track 17

J ▸ Joanne，C ▸ Mr. Chang，R ▸ Reservation

C: Hi, um... My mom is in Brisbane, and she's critically ill in hospital... I have a ticket but it's for the day after tomorrow. Would you help me to get home immediately? I'm sorry, but it's really urgent. Please!

J: I see. May I have your passport and ticket please? We'll make a contact with our reservation department and see if there is a seat for you.

C: Okay, please, thank you.

(Making a phone call)

J: Hello, this is Joanne from Kaohsiung airport. We have a passenger who has a ticket from Kaohsiung to Brisbane via Hong Kong on the day after tomorrow. The ticket number is 043-898832456. It's extremely urgent for him to see his mother who is in hospital, so please help him to find a seat, thank you.

R: Okay. The flights today are fully booked... maybe we have to wait until someone cancel.

J: Okay. Now we still have seats on XX455 and XX 457 to Hong Kong. All we need is a seat for ongoing flight to Brisbane.

R: Okay. I'll keep on finding a seat for Mr. Chang here. If there is any available, I'll let you know, cheers.

(Hang up the phone)

C: How is it?

J: Sir, there is no seat from Hong Kong to Brisbane now, but we'll try our best to find a seat for you.

(10 minutes later, the phone rings)

R: Hi, Joanne. I found a seat on XX157, but it's Y class. The ticket Mr. Chang has is S class, so he needs to pay $12,000. Please ask him if it's okay.

J: Mr. Chang, good news! We found a seat for you, but it will charge you about $12,000, is it okay?

C: Oh! Thank you! Sure! Just tell me what I should do!

J: Please talk to our reservation. She'll tell you. (Hand in the phone)

R: Hello, Mr. Chang. The seat has already booked for you now.

Do you have your credit card with you? Please read the card number for me.

C: Okay... 4658-8888-9999-1234.

R: The expiry date?

C: March 2018.

R: Thank you. Sir, the card has been verified. Your booking is successfully done.

Memo

C: 嗨，嗯…我母親現在在布里斯本，現在在醫院病危…我有張票但是是後天的票…所以…你可以幫我讓我現在馬上回家嗎？我很抱歉，但這真的很急。麻煩你！

J: 我了解了。可以給我您的護照跟機票嗎？我們會聯絡訂位組，看是不是有位子。

C: 好的，拜託了，謝謝你。

（打電話）

J: 哈囉，我是高雄機場的 Joanne。我們有位乘客持有後天的機票從高雄經香港到布里斯本。機票號碼是 043-898832456。他非常急著回去看他媽媽，他媽媽人在醫院，所以麻煩幫忙找一個位子，謝謝。

R: 好的。嗯…今天的航班都訂滿了，也許我們要等到有人取消。

J: 好的。我們現在 XX455 跟 XX457 都還有座位。我們只需要後段往布里斯本的飛機座位。

R: 好的。我會繼續幫張先生找位子。如果有任何位子釋出，我會跟你說，謝啦。

（掛掉電話）

C: 結果如何？

J: 先生，現在香港到布里斯本沒有位子，但請等候好消息。我們會盡力幫您找到座位。

（10 分鐘後，電話響）

J: 哈囉，Speedy 航空。

R: 嗨，Joanne。我剛找到一個位子在 XX157，但是 Y 艙。張先生的票是 S 艙，所以要付 12,000 元噢。請你問他這樣可以嗎？

J: 張先生，好消息！我們幫您找到一個位子，但要收 12,000 元，這樣可以嗎？

C: 噢！謝謝！可以！當然！你只要跟我說怎麼做就好！

J: 請跟我們訂位組電話上談，她會告訴你。（將電話交給他）

R: 你好，張先生。已經幫您將位子訂好了。

C: 謝謝！謝謝！那我現在要做什麼？

R: 請有帶您的信用卡嗎？請將您的卡號唸給我。

C: 好的…4658-8888-9999-1234。

R: 有效日期是？

C: 2018 年 3 月。

R: 謝謝您。先生，這裡已經接受您的刷卡了。您的定位已經成功。

英文母語者這麼說

Would you help me to get home immediately?

（你可以幫助我馬上回家嗎？）

上面這句使用 get 有種「到達」的感覺。不要說 Would you help me to go home immediately?這樣說起來有點像是迷路了，需要人家幫你找路。若要使用 go 這個動詞，則改為 Would you help me going back home?用動名詞代替 to go home。

The flights today are fully booked.
（今天的航班都訂滿了。）

不說 The flights today are full booking，我們習慣說 booking 表示「訂位」，所以也很容易帶到英文裡，「訂位滿了」就會變成 full booking，工作時其實大家都聽得懂，但按英文文法來說應該是 fully booked。

字彙解析

- **critically** *adv.* 危急地
  His father is critically ill.（他爸爸病危。）
- **reservation** *n.* 訂位
  He made a reservation for valentine's Day.（他為了過情人節訂了位。）
- **verify** *v.* 證實、證明；查清；這裡用來指證實本人刷了信用卡
  The transaction has been verified.（這筆交易已經證實成功了。）

補充片語

❶ make a contact with 與…聯絡

例 Would you make a contact with Mr. Huang?（可以請你與黃先生聯絡嗎？）

解 contact 本句中當名詞使用，要加上 with，前面的 make 才是本句的動詞。

❷ keep on 繼續（動作）

例 Keep on going, we haven't reached the goal.（繼續走，我們還沒抵達終點。）

解 keep on 是「繼續一個動作」的意思，後面的動詞必須加上 ing 變成動名詞。如文中「繼續尋找座位」就是 keep on finding a seat。

❸ cheers 謝啦

例 A: Would you like some beer? B: Oh, yes. Cheers.（A：你要來點啤酒嗎？B：喔，好。謝啦。）

解 此用法較常見於英式英語，為「謝謝」的意思，因為很口語，所以這邊翻成「謝啦」，感覺比較像。

In Other Words

❶ All we need is a seat for ongoing flight to Brisbane. = The only thing we need is a seat for ongoing flight to Brisbane.（我們只需要後段班機到布里斯本的座位。）

解 All someone need is 是指「某人只需要的是」，故作另一說法為 the only thing someone need is～。

❷ I will let you know. = I will tell you. = I'll pass the message on to you.（我會告知你。）

解 這也是有很多說法的一句話，上述三種皆可以表示「我會告知你」。

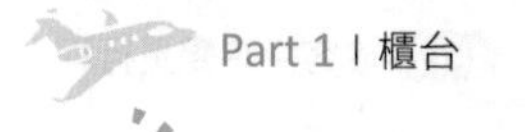

地勤工作解說

在機場工作，一定會遇到各種狀況。這一篇是真實發生過的案例。關於艙等，各家航空給的艙等代號不盡相同。以筆者所待的公司而言，S 艙及 Y 艙都是經濟艙，但是依照票種不同又分出次艙等，也就是不同規定的票，如有些票可以免費改日期、有些若 no show（搭機當天沒有出現在機場）要付費。一般來說，最貴的票擁有最大的彈性。因此文中張先生最後補 12000 元買的就是票面價最有彈性的 Y 艙機票。

前輩經驗巧巧說

在機場，為了管理辦理登機的速度，必須讓辦理登機的櫃檯進出保持流暢，如前面提到，沒有問題的話，每一位乘客辦理登機約 2-3 分鐘即可完成，若遇到乘客有任何問題卡住，都會影響到辦理登機的速度，因而影響航班起飛時間。因此，每家航空公司除了辦理登機的櫃檯以外，還有一個 information 櫃檯，專門處理登機以外，如機票問題、訂位問題、改名字、超重收費等無法在一般櫃檯解決的事情。information 櫃檯扮演極為重要的角色，處理各式疑難雜症，通常都要有一定經驗及特質的人才有辦法做好這個位子喔！

1-18 旅客特殊服務：餐飲

情境介紹

旅客 Peter 於訂位時需求特殊餐點服務。

情境對話 Track 18

J ▸ Joanna，P ▸ Peter

J: Hello, sir. This is Speedy Air. How can I help you?

P: I have already booked my flight on 19 October, and I would like to request a special meal.

J: Okay, sir. Can I have your reservation number?

P: It's 5ZRPK.

J: Thank you. Ok, I find your booking record. May I confirm the schedule with you, the flight is from Taipei taking a transfer via Singapore to the final destination Sydney?

P: Yes.

J: What is the special meal you would like to have?

P: Vegetarian meal, please.

J: We offer various meals for vegetarian passengers, such as

Indian, Vegetarian Meal, Vegetarian Lacto-Ovo Meal, Vegetarian Oriental Meal, and Vegetarian Vegan Meal.

P: What's the difference of the meals?

J: Let me explain the ingredients of these veggie meals to you. For Indian Vegetarian Meal is made by spicy vegetarian combinations, with limited use of dairy products. Vegetarian Lacto-Ovo Meal is included high in protein, iron and calcium, along with dairy products, eggs and vegetarian-type of cheese. Vegetarian Oriental Meal is prepared in Chinese style, along with fruits and vegetables. No meat, poultry, fish, seafood, eggs, dairy products, roots or bulbous vegetables including ginger, garlic, onion, spring onions. Vegetarian Vegan Meal is strict vegetarian food with high protein, rich iron and high calcium.

P: I choose Vegetarian Oriental Meal.

J: No problem. May I confirm your special meal is for whole journey or only for one sector?

P: For the whole journey.

J: OK, sir. The Vegetarian Oriental Meal has been requested successfully.

P: Thank you, bye.

譯文

J: 先生，您好。這裡是速達航空，有什麼可以幫你的嗎？

P: 我已訂了十月十九的機票，而我想需求特別餐。

J: 好的，麻煩請您給我預定編號嗎？

P: 5ZRPK。

J: 謝謝。我已查到您的訂位紀錄。這邊跟您確認一下行程，請問是從台北飛往新加坡再到目的地雪梨嗎？

P: 沒錯。

J: 請問需求哪一種特別餐？

P: 素食餐。

J: 我們提供乘客不同種類的素食餐，例如：印度素食、西式乳蛋類素食、中式素食以及嚴格西式素食。

P: 有什麼不同呢？

J: 跟您說明這些素食餐的內容物。印度素食是由印度式辛辣素食餐，可含少量乳類製品組成。西式乳蛋類素食餐含豐富蛋白質、鐵質及鈣質，可含乳類製品，雞蛋及不含凝乳酵素的乳酪。中式素食餐，是含蔬果，不含肉類、家禽、魚類、海產、蛋、乳類製品、根或球根類植物（薑、蒜、洋蔥及蔥）。嚴格西式素食餐是嚴格素食材料，含豐富蛋白質、鐵質及鈣質。

P: 我選中式素食。

J: 沒問題，請問你的素食餐世全程都需求還是只需要其中一段航程？

P: 全程都需要素食餐。

J: 好的，已成功幫您訂好中式

P: 謝謝你。

英文母語者這麼說

麻煩可以給我預訂您的預訂編號嗎？

中式英文 Give me your reservation number.

正確用法 Can I have your reservation number?

> 此句從中文字面上直翻並沒有錯誤，但口氣上顯得不禮貌，服務業用語如果需要對方提供資訊通常都會用 Can I have... or May I have.....?

這些餐點有何不同呢？

中式英文 What is the different meals?

正確用法 What is the difference of the meals?

> 上述中式英文的句子意思是『這些不同的餐點是什麼？』這樣與本對話所要表達的完全不同，整句的重點是「不同之處」變成主要名詞，因此正確說法為 What is the difference of the meals?

字彙解析

- **vegetarian** *adj.* 吃素的；素食的 *n.* 素食主義者

  This restaurant offers a variety of meals for vegetarian.（這家餐廳提供給素食者多樣化的餐點。）

- **lacto** *n.* 乳糖；乳酸

  The diet of Lacto-ovo vegetarians excludes meat and fish but includes eggs and diary products.（蛋奶素食者是排除肉類和魚類，而吃蛋和乳製品。）

- **poultry** *n.* 家禽

  The most common poultry is chicken.（公雞是最常見的家禽。）

- **bulbous** *adj.* 球根的；球跟狀的

  Onions leeks chives garlic and shallots belong to bulbous plants.（洋蔥、韭蔥、細香蔥、大蒜和青蔥是屬於球莖植物。）

- **protein** *n.* 蛋白質 *adj.* 蛋白質的

  Insufficient intake in protein makes Angela's body so weak.（安琪拉因為蛋白攝取不足而身體太虛弱。）

- **calcium** *n.* 鈣

  The elderly need more calcium to prevent osteoporosis.（老人家需要多攝取鈣來預防骨質疏鬆症。）

補充片語

❶ with limited use 少量使用

例 Using fewer plastic bags when shopping is what our government advocates.（我們的政府提倡購物時請少量使用塑膠袋。）

解 with limited use 後面通常用 of 來接名詞，藉以強調此名詞為整句的主角

❷ along with 包含

例 The ingredients of this juice is avocado, along with apple, grapes, and passionfruits.（這杯果汁的內容物為酪梨、蘋果、葡萄、百香果。）

解 在此篇對話中是指餐點的內容物包含可作為 include 替換詞，但 along with 也有『與…一起』的意思。

In Other Words

❶ I have already booked my flight.

=My flight reservation has been made.（我已經訂好機票了。）

解 對話中的句子是以人當為主詞較為直述的用法，如要強調訂位已成功可改為被動式，將訂位當成主詞來凸顯

❷ We offer various meals for vegetarian passengers.

= A variety of vegetarian meals are provided to passengers.

（我們提供多樣化的餐點給素食旅客者。）

解 如果以多種餐點當作主詞，就必須要用被動式句型，被動式可用來強調物品的重要性。而對話中沒用被動式句子，是想來突顯航空公司能夠提供多選擇給乘客，主角是航空公司而非餐點。

地勤工作解說

一般航空公司規定如需特殊餐飲，最晚必須要在航班起飛 24 小時前完成訂餐，旅客可在訂位時向旅行社說或在網路訂位系統自行加註餐飲服務，此項服務是完全免費。至機場櫃台劃位時，地勤人員會向旅客再次確認特殊餐點是否正確。

前輩經驗巧巧說

特殊餐點服務可分為四大類別：素食餐點、醫療病理餐、宗教信仰餐點、兒童或嬰兒餐。其中較特別的餐點如醫療病理餐點，可提供糖尿病餐、低卡路里餐、低脂餐、低鹽餐、低乳糖餐；宗教信仰餐則分為猶太教餐、印度教餐、伊斯蘭教餐。特殊餐點都會經過較處理時間與特殊烹調方式，因此航空公司才希望旅客能在航班起飛前 24 小時訂好餐點，且旅客如在劃位櫃檯臨時想取消或加訂特別餐，航空公司是無法即時提供給旅客的。另外，每項特殊餐點都會有英文代碼，如中式素食餐點為 VOML、兒童餐 CHML、低卡路里餐 LCML、猶太教餐 KSML，航空公司人員會運用英文代碼加註在訂位系統中。

1-19 旅客特殊服務：嬰兒車

情境介紹

一位媽媽帶 3 歲兒童搭機經香港轉機前往英國倫敦，攜帶一輛嬰兒車。

情境對話 Track 19

M ▸ Mom，J ▸ Jason

J: Good morning, Madam. May I have your passports, please? Thank you.

(Handing in the passports)

J: May I confirm your itinerary with you, are you traveling to London via Hong Kong?

M: Yes.

J: Would you like to check in your baby stroller here or do you want use it until the boarding gate?

M: What is the difference?

J: If you would like to have your stroller to the boarding gate, we will tag your stroller with a baggage tag and shipside an offload tag here, and collect it before boarding.

M: Can I have it in Hong Kong?

J: No problem, please wait at the arrival gate. Our colleague in Hong Kong will return the cart to you.

M: What if I check in the cart at the counter?

J: If you check it in here, you will be unable to have it in Hong Kong; you need to collect it in London at the baggage carousel.

M: I think my son would like to have his cart to the boarding gate, thank you.

J: No problem. These are your boarding passes. Please arrive at the gate before the time written on the boarding pass, thank you.

譯文

J: 您好，總共兩位同行嗎？麻煩兩位的護照，謝謝。

（遞護照）

J: 跟您確認您的行程是經香港轉機至倫敦嗎？

M: 是的。

J: 請問您的嬰兒車要在這裏托運或是使用到登機門？

M: 有什麼不一樣嗎？

J: 如果您想讓小朋友坐嬰兒車至登機門，我們會在這裡幫您的嬰兒車掛上行李條及機邊托運掛牌，登機前我們再幫您收起來托運。

M: 那我在香港轉機時可以取出來使用嗎？

J: 沒有問題，您下飛機後，請在出口處稍待，香港地勤人員會將嬰兒車交給您。

M: 那如果在櫃檯直接托運呢？

J: 在這裡托運的話，在香港轉機時就無法拿到您的嬰兒車了，需在倫敦行李轉盤領取。

M: 我想我兒子會想坐他的車到登機門，謝謝。

J: 沒問題，這是您的登機證，請於登機證上所寫的時間前抵達登機門，謝謝您。

英文母語者這麼說

Are you traveling to London via Hong Kong?

（您今天經香港轉機至倫敦嗎？）

不說 Are you traveling to London “transit” via Hong Kong?通常「轉機」若使用 via 已經有轉機的意思在裡面，不用特別在說一次 transit。

字彙解析

- **itinerary** *n.* 行程，路線

  The destination on my itinerary is wrong, would you please check it for me?（我行程表上的目的地是錯的，可以請你幫我查查嗎？）

- **baby stroller** 嬰兒車；娃娃車

  The baby stroller was bought in Japan.（這嬰兒車是在日本買的。）

- **tag** *v.* 給…掛上標籤

  My baggage was tagged with wrong destination by your ground staff in Hong Kong, how can I find it back?（我的行李被你們香港的地勤掛錯目的地了，我要怎麼找回來？）

- **shipside** *n.* 機邊（飛機旁邊的區域）

  Some jobs around shipside are dangerous, you need license to work there.（有些機邊的工作很危險，你需要考過證照才能在那裏工作。）

- **offload** *v.* 卸下，卸（貨），下（客），拉掉（客人）

  The old lady at 53D is too nervous for flight; we need to offload her and her baggage.（坐在 53D 的老太太情緒太過緊張不能飛行，我們得將她拉掉並卸下她的行李。）

- **baggage carousel** 行李轉盤

The baggage carousel is stuck, please stay outside the yellow line in case it starts to work suddenly.（行李轉盤卡住了，請在黃線外等候，以免它突然開始運轉。）

補充片語

❶ what if ....？ 如果…的話呢？

例 What if I check in the cart at the counter?（如果我在櫃檯托運嬰兒車的話呢？）

解 想要詢問「如果～的話，會如何呢？」英文可以使用 what if …? 如上述情境中乘客的嬰兒車託運有兩種選擇：在機邊下行李或是在櫃檯托運。地勤 Jill 解釋過第一種之後，乘客想知道另一種選擇「如果在櫃檯托運的話」會是怎樣的情況呢？可以說 What if I check in the cart at the counter?

❷ check something in; check in something 將…托運

解 這裏要說明的是 check something in 與 check in something 的差別。check something in 的 something 通常是使用「代名詞」，check in something 的 something 則是物品名稱。所以第一次提到要托運嬰兒車，請說 check in the baby stroller，之後再次提及托運嬰兒車時，因為前面已經提過，不再重複，可說 check it in。

In Other Words

❶ If you would like to have your stroller to the boarding gate, we will tag your stroller with a baggage tag and shipside offload tag here, and collect it before boarding. = You can have your stroller until the boarding gate and offload it there if you wish to use it, and we will tag it with a baggage tag and shipside offload tag here.

地勤工作解說

當乘客伴有嬰兒或兒童同行並攜帶有嬰兒車時，上飛機前須先將嬰兒車託運。託運可以選擇要在櫃檯與其他行李一同託運，直接從櫃檯後方輸送帶送往貨艙。但考量小朋友的需求，許多家長希望在登機前都可以使用嬰兒車。因此，通常攜帶有嬰兒車的乘客都會選擇到登機門再將嬰兒車託運。此時，必須先於櫃檯將行李條及「機邊下行李掛牌」掛上嬰兒車，表示這台嬰兒車在登機門前要收起來送到貨艙。

前輩經驗巧巧說

記得剛進航空公司，在登機門邊學姊們就會交代「今天有一台娃娃車，先去看看他們到登機門了沒，如果到了先去把娃娃車收起來。」（導致後來有點職業病，在路上看到娃娃車都會想去幫它收起來。）因為在機邊下的行李與在櫃台託運不同，必須在登機門邊交由貨運部同事手提到飛機側邊上飛機，這是一段不算近的距離，且因必須在乘客上飛機前完成所有行李的安置，為了不造成飛機延誤，只要負責的該班機有嬰兒車，在所有乘客完成報到手續後，督導會藉由無線電提醒登機門同事；登機門同事也會利用電腦系統查詢該航班共有幾台娃娃車，確保所有工作能準時完成。印象中，最高紀錄是一班飛機有 6 台娃娃車要收，同事們對各式各樣嬰兒車都已練就 3 秒收起嬰兒車的本領。通常航空公司會提供一個大塑膠袋將嬰兒車包好，綁起來，以防在運輸過程被弄濕（比方在轉機時剛好遇到當地下大雨）。若乘客需轉機，常常也希望在轉機機場可以使用嬰兒車，此時除了如上述要將嬰兒車掛上行李掛牌及機邊下行李掛牌外，在辦公室的同事會協助發送電報給轉機航站的同事，告知該班飛機將有嬰兒車要在轉機航站使用嬰兒車（也因此嬰兒車會放置在貨艙靠進出口處），請他們為乘客服務。

1-20 旅客特殊服務：輪椅

情境介紹

行動不便旅客 Andy 在機場劃位櫃台需求輪椅服務。

情境對話 Track 20

M ▸ Mary，A ▸ Andy

M: Good afternoon, sir. Where are you traveling to today?

A: Hi, Madam. I am going to Boston via Tokyo.

M: Ok, may I have your passport?

A: Here is my passport. Can I make a request? I need a wheelchair service. My left ankle is twisted yesterday.

M: Sure, we can provide a wheelchair to you. Are you able to ascend and descend steps?

A: I'm afraid not.

M: Do you require wheelchair assistance to ascend and descend the aircraft and walk to your seat?

A: No, thank you.

M: Are you going to use your own wheelchair?

A: No, I don't have my own wheelchair.

M: Do you need this service during a part of your trip or the whole trip?

A: The whole trip, please. Oh, including the flight transfer.

M: Ok, no problem. We've marked out that in your booking record. Here are your boarding passes and the assistance card.

A: What is the assistance card?

M: When you are on board, you're going to need a wheelchair service up on arrival. You could show this card to our cabin crew, meaning you need wheelchair service on arrival.

A: Ok, I see.

M: Sir, please have a seat next to our counter. The wheelchair will be ready in 5 minutes. Then our staff will help you to the boarding gate.

A: Thanks for your kind help.

M: You're welcome. Have a nice trip.

譯文

M:先生，午安。請問今天要前往哪裡呢？

A: 嗨，我今天經東京轉機到波士頓。

M:好的，跟您借一下護照？

A: 這是我的護照。我可以有個請求嗎？昨天因為我的腳踝扭傷了，我需要輪椅服務。

M:當然沒問題。我們可以提供輪椅給您。請問您能上下台階嗎？

A: 我恐怕沒辦法。

M:從機艙門到您的座位以及上下台階需要輪椅協助嗎？

A: 不需要，謝謝。

M:您要用自己的輪椅嗎？

A: 不，我沒有自己的輪椅。

M:您是整段航程還是其中一段航程都需要輪椅服務？

A: 整趟旅程我都需要輪椅服務包含轉機時。

M:好的，沒問題。我們已經在您的訂位紀錄裡註明好輪椅需求。這是您的登機證與協助卡。

A: 這張協助卡是什麼？

M:當您上飛機時，請出示此張協助卡給空服員，表示在您抵達目的地時需要輪椅服務。

A: 好的，我明白了。

M:先生麻煩您先在櫃檯旁的椅子稍坐一下。五分鐘後我們將準備好您的輪椅，然後我們的工作人員會協助您到登機門。

A: 謝謝您的幫忙。

英文母語者這麼說

從機艙門到您的座位以及上下台階需要輪椅協助嗎？

中式英文：Do you need help wheelchair from aircraft to your seat?

正確說法：Do you require wheelchair assistance to ascend and descend the aircraft and walk to your seat?

> 這樣寫法會變成「你需要幫忙輪椅嗎？」雖從字面以及文法上看似正確，但句意完全錯誤。正確應該把『輪椅協助』當成副詞為 *wheelchair assistance*，且上述中式英文句子沒有提到上下台階，也不正確。

當您上飛機時…

中式英文：When you go to airplane...

正確說法：When you are on board...

> 如果用 *go to airplane* 意思會變成當您走向飛機，並沒有強調登機。通常登機、登船的英文為 *on board*。

字彙解析

- **ankle** *n.* 腳踝

  Simon's ankle is sprained since he fell heavily.（Simon 的腳踝扭傷了因為他摔了一大跤。）

- **wheelchair** *n.* 輪椅

  My grandfather needs wheelchair because he is too old to walk long distance.（我的爺爺需要輪椅因為他年紀太大無法走太遠。）

- **twist** *v.* 扭傷；轉動

  He slipped on the floor and twisted his knee.（他在地板上滑倒而扭傷膝蓋。）

- **require** *v.* 需要；要求

  If you require further information, please contact to our company.（如果你需要多資訊，請與我們公司聯絡。）

- **aircraft** *n.* 飛機；機型

  The aircraft flying to New York is Boeing 747.（飛往紐約的這架飛機是波音 747。）

- **assistance** *n.* 協助；援助

  Joanne finished this project without any assistance.（Joanne 在沒人任何協助之下完成這份專案。）

補充片語

❶ on board 登機；登船

例 **Mr. Yang will bring a crutch on board.**（楊先生將會攜帶拐杖登機。）

解 **board** 原本是動詞上船、上車、上飛機的意思，前面加個 **on** 變成片語後，就可省略後面接交通工具。

❷ on arrival 抵達

例 **We need the shuttle bus on arrival because we have much baggage.**（抵達時我們需要接駁車接送因為我們又太多的行李了。）

解 **arrival** 前面加個介詞 **on** 當成片語「抵達」某地，通常我們會說 **arrive in Sydney**，但直接用 **on arrival** 後面可直接省略目的地，避免文章中一直重複寫地名。

In Other Words

❶ I need a wheelchair service because I twisted my left ankle yesterday.＝ Owing to my sprained ankle I would like to request a wheelchair service.（昨天因為我的腳踝扭傷了，我需要輪椅服務。）

解 Owing to 是「由於」的意思，強調由於什麼樣的緣故而造成的。另外 sprain 也是扭傷等同於 twist 用法。

❷ When you are on board the aircraft, you could show this card to our cabin crew that means you need wheelchair service on arrival. ＝This assistance card could be presented once you are on board this flight that means you require a wheelchair service on arrival.（當您上飛機時，出示此張協助卡給空服員即表示在您抵達目的地時需要輪椅服務。）

解 Once 可作為「當…時」＝when 的用法，且可將協助卡當主詞強調其重要性。present 出示比起用 show 更為正式說法。

地勤工作解說

旅客可在訂機票時或是在機場劃位櫃檯需求輪椅服務。一般來說，航空公司將輪椅服務分為三種類型及其代碼：WCHR、WCHS、WCHR。地勤會向旅客詢問一些問題藉此來判斷該輪椅旅客是屬於哪種類型。WCHR 為旅客能上下台階並且能在機艙內行動，只是需要輪椅從劃位櫃檯到機艙門口。WCHS 的旅客則是無法上下台階但可自行移動從機艙門口到座位上。WCHC 是旅客完全無法自行移動，需求輪椅從外面一直到機艙內的座位上。

前輩經驗巧巧說

輪椅服務是旅客特殊服務中最為重要的項目之一，我們必須提供給行動不便的旅客在旅程中最好的服務。大部份的旅客如有輪椅需求，會在訂位時也一併加註輪椅服務，所以當旅客來到櫃檯劃位時，就可從訂位紀錄中看到是屬於哪種類型的輪椅旅客。然而，地勤劃位時需格外留意訂位記錄中的輪椅代碼是否與旅客的真實狀況相符，有時會發現旅客的狀態比訂位記錄中的輪椅級別更加嚴重。另外，旅客是否使用自己的輪椅，並需注意該輪椅為手動或電動輪椅，手動輪椅可讓客人使用到機艙門口，再由工作人員在收取放入行李貨艙。如有電動輪椅需托運，電池必須和輪椅分開拆除並且須將電池做好絕緣包裝，並且需通知貨運部及機長，該輪椅的電池存放在哪個貨倉位置，因為大多數電動輪椅的電池為鋰電池，鋰電池是屬於飛航的危險物品之一，需特別留意。

1-21 單獨旅行的兒童

情境介紹

一位王太太打至訂位組幫她的 10 歲兒子訂票，從台北至洛杉磯。

情境對話 Track 21

J ▸ Jason，W ▸ Mrs. Wang

W: Hi, I want to book the flight for my 10-year-old son.

J: Hello, Madam. Will you accompany your children for traveling?

W: No, I won't travel with my son.

J: I see. Let me advise you that children who travel alone who are aged 6 to under 12 years must be registered as Unaccompanied Minors(UM) to ensure the safety of children traveling alone. Our airport staff will care for your child throughout the journey, such as escorting your son through immigration, keep the passport and documents for him and give his passport to cabin crew when boarding. Then, our ground staff will accompany him until he is collected by the nominated adult at the arriving airport.

W: Is there extra fees will be paid for this service?

J: Yes, the surcharges will be applied for this service, and It's based on sector. Where's your child going to?

W: He's going to Los Angeles from Taipei on November 25 and he'll be back on December 30. Please book economy class for him.

J: No problem. I find one flight S743, the departure time at Taipei is 7:00am and the arrival time is 19:00. The return flight S740 on 30 December that is departed from Los Angeles at 11:00 and arrival time is 22:30 in Taipei. The ticket is TWD 38,000 and UM fee is TWD 2,000. The total of this journey is TWD 40,000. Is this schedule suitable for your son?

W: Yes, it's great. Please make this reservation. I'll pay by credit card.

J: Ok. Please tell me your child name, the contact detail of you and the responsible person meeting your son at airport in Los Angeles.

W: (saying the details to Joy)

J: Thank you, Mrs. Wang. I'll send the UM form to our office at Taipei airport. This form is included all contact details about the authorized person to pick up your child and you. When you accompany your son to check-in counter, our staff will double check the details with you. UM form will be kept with your son's passport on our staff hand. One more thing to remind you that the responsible person meeting your child must provide proof of identification before your son is handed over.

譯文

W: 嗨，我想要幫我 10 歲的兒子訂機票。

J: 您好，女士。請問您將會陪您的孩子旅行嗎？

W: 不，我不會與他一起旅行。

J: 好的，我瞭解。跟您説明一下年滿六歲至未滿十二歲的獨自旅行的兒童，必須登記為『單獨搭機旅行的未成年人』以確保孩童獨自旅行的安全。我們機場的員工將全程照顧您的小孩，例如陪同您的兒子通過移民署護照查驗、保管他的護照和文件當登機時再轉交給空服員。當抵達目的地機場時，地勤人員將陪同他直到指定的成年人來接他為止。

W: 針對此項服務有額外的費用嗎？

J: 是，此項服務將有相關費用產生，會就所搭乘的航段來計算。請問您的小孩將前往哪裡呢？

W: 他將在 11 月 25 號出發前往洛杉磯，然後於 12 月 30 號回來。麻煩幫他訂經濟艙。

J: 沒問題。我查到一個航班 S743，台北起飛時間為上午七點然後到達時間為晚上七點。從洛杉磯回程的航班，起飛時間是上午十一點，抵達台北時間為晚上十點半。機票價格為台幣三萬八，而『單獨搭機的未成年人』費用是台幣兩千。此趟行程的費用總共為台幣四萬元。請問這行程適合您兒子嗎？

W: 明白了，請幫我兒子訂位。我將用信用卡支付。

J: 好的，謝謝您。請告訴我您小孩的名字和您的，與負責在洛杉磯機場接您兒子的聯絡資料。

W:（告訴訂票人員聯絡資料中）

J: 感謝您，王太太。我將寄送『單獨搭機旅行的未成年人』表格到我們台北機場辦公室。這個表格內容包含了您和指定接機的親友聯絡資料。當您陪同您兒子到劃位櫃檯時，我們的地勤人員將會再次向您核對資料。『單獨搭機旅行的未成年人』表格和您兒子的護照將會被我們工作人員所保管。再次提醒您，負責接您兒子的人必須向我們提供身份證明文件，才能接走您小孩。

英文母語者這麼說

（針對此項服務有額外的費用嗎？）

中式英文：Is there extra money for this service?

正確說法：Is there extra fees will be paid for this service?

「額外費用」就字面上直翻 extra money 看起來好像沒錯，但「費用」的英文單字可用 fee，正式說法應為 extra fee 而非 extra money。此外，此句中式英文也少了動詞「付費」，雖然中文可以省略不寫，但英文句型結構必須要完整，因此要用 pay 此動詞表達「付費」，而且須為被動式。

字彙解析

- **unaccompanied** *adj.* 無伴隨的；無伴侶的

  I will attend this party unaccompanied since my husband has a meeting tomorrow.（我將獨自一人參加這場派對因為我丈夫明天要開會。）

- **minor** *n.* 未成年人

  Serving drinks and cigarettes to minors is illegal.（販售酒和香菸給未成年人是違法的。）

- **register** *v.* 登記;註冊

  He registered this house in his wife's name.（他登記這棟房子在他太太的名下。）

- **nominate** *v.* 指定；提名

  Gary is nominated as the candidate in the next election.（蓋瑞被提名為下屆選舉的候選人。）

- **escort** *v.* 護送

  Peter would like to escort this girl home.（彼得想要護送這位女生回家。）

- **surcharge** *n.* 附加費用；額外費

  If you forget to pay this bill before 30th December, the surcharges will be made.（如果你忘記在十二月三十號前付清帳單，將會有額外費用。）

- **authorized** *adj.* 經授權的

The secretary is the authorized person by our CEO to enter this accountant office.（這位秘書是經我們的執行長授權可以進出這間財務室的人。）

- **proof** *n.* 證明；證據

Please find out the proof who stole the jewels.（請找出證據誰是偷了珠寶的人。）

補充片語

❶ pick up 接某人

例 Please arrive the airport at 17:00 for picking up our client.（請於下午五點時到達機場接我們的客戶。）

In Other Words

❶ Our ground staff will accompany him until he is collected by the nominated adult at arriving airport. = Our ground staff will keep him company until he met up the adult you designated on arrival.（地勤人員將陪同他直到指定的成年人來接他為止。）

解 accompany 可用另一個片語 keep sb. company 來替代也是陪伴某人的意思。片語「met up 見面」用於替換句型內傳達出指定成年人於機場見面後接走小孩的意思。

❷ One more thing to remind you that the responsible person meeting your child must provide proof of identification before your son is handed over. = I may remind you that the accountable adult meeting your child must present the ID before your son is hand over.（再提醒您一件事，負責接您兒子的人必須向我們提供身份證明文件，才能接走您小孩。）

解 One more thing remind you 可直接說 I may remind you，accountable 則相等於 responsible「負責的」。請向我們提供身分證件英文可用 present the ID，present 出示的意思。

地勤工作解說

為了確保 12 歲以下的未成年人單獨旅行的安全，航空公司提供了UM的特殊服務，但須在班機起飛 24 小時前向當地訂位組申請此項服務，不能於出發當天臨時需求，費用會依據所搭乘的航段來收取，每家航空公司費用不盡相同。如行程內有轉機，轉機時間則不能超過五小時。

前輩經驗巧巧說

在機場劃位櫃檯辦理「UM 單獨旅行的未成年人」時，必須向陪同孩童前來的成年人收取 UM 表格並仔細核對抵達目的地之指定聯絡人資料，且安排孩童坐於前排位置，以便航行時空服人員能隨時留意照顧孩童。地勤人員在轉交孩童給空服員時都會確實在 UM 表格內簽名以示負責，也會與下個工作人員確認保管孩童的哪些證件。抵達目的地後，協助孩童通關領取行李後，地勤人員必須核對指定聯絡人的身分證件與表格內容是否相符，確認無誤後才能將未成年人轉交，以免孩童被不認識的人接走。

1-22 18 歲以下無父母陪同前往南非

情境介紹

一位澳洲籍爺爺帶 6 歲孫子搭機前往南非，未帶齊所需的文件（缺該兒童的父母表示同意該兒童外遊的宣誓證明），無法當天出發。

情境對話 Track 22

J ‣ Joanne，G ‣ Grandpa

J: Good evening, Sir. Where is your final destination?

G: Johannesburg.

J: Two people traveling today?

G: Yes, with my grandson.

J: May I have your passports, please? Thank you.

(Handing in the passports)

J: May I explain to you, if you are traveling with children without their parents, some documents are needed, such as a copy of the children's birth certificate, an affidavit from the parents or legal guardians, stating consent to travel, copies of identification documents of parents or legal guardians, and contact details of parents or legal guardians. Do you have these documents in English with you?

G: Oh, yes, yes....here are the documents.

J: Ok, Let me check for you. Oh! if there is no affidavit from the parents, the immigration office of South Africa will refuse your landing.

G: Oh! What should I do?

J: Let me check your ticket to see if it is available to change the date.

G: Please, thank you.

J: No problem, it is free for re-booking your flight. No charge will be needed.

G: How can I re-book the flight?

J: Please get the document ready, and call up our reservation center. Here is the number.

G: Ok, thank you.

譯文

J: 您好，請問目的地到哪裡？

G: 約翰尼斯堡。

J: 總共兩位同行嗎？

G: 是，和孫子一起。

J: 好的，麻煩兩位的護照，謝謝。

（遞護照）

J: 跟您說明一下，帶小朋友去南非，若非父母同行，需要一些文件，像出生證明副本、父母或監護人同意小朋友出國的宣誓證明、父母或監護人的身分證明文件副本與父母或監護人的連絡資料。請問有準備好這些英文版的文件在身上嗎？

G: 噢，有，有…在這裡。

J: 嗯，我幫您看一下…少了爸媽同意小朋友出國的宣誓證明，這樣南非移民處不會讓您入境。

G: 那怎麼辦？

J: 我幫您看看您的機票是否可以改期。

G: 麻煩你。

J: 沒問題，重新訂位是免費，您不需再付任何費用。

G: 要怎麼重新訂位呢？

J: 請您先準備好這些文件，再打電話跟訂位組改日期。這是訂位組的電話，提供給您。

G: 好的，謝謝。

英文母語者這麼說

Do you have these documents in English with you?

（請問有準備好這些英文版的文件在身上嗎？）

非 *Do you prepare these documents in English with you*，文法上沒錯，但重點在於「帶在身上」不在「準備」，習慣上會使用 *have* 當動詞帶過，取代 *prepare*。

字彙解析

- **destination** *n.* 目的地

  Where is your destination today?（今天的目的地是哪裡呢？）

- **affidavit** *n.* 宣誓書

  Please provide your affidavit to the lawyer.（請提供你的宣誓書給律師。）

- **legal guardian** *n.* 法定監護人

  Here needs the signature of her legal guardian.（這裡要請她的法定監護人簽名。）

- **consent** *n.* 同意書

  We need you to sign the consent to ensure the surgery is under family's approval.（我們需要你在這同意書上簽名，以確保這手術是經過家人同意的。）

- **re-book** *v.* 重新訂位

  If you didn't catch this flight, you will be charge $600 to re-book the flight.（如果你沒搭上這班飛機，重新訂位需要收取 600 元的費用。）

- **refuse landing** 拒絕入境

  He forgot to apply the visa, so the immigration had refused his landing.（他忘了申請簽證，所以移民官拒絕讓他入境。）

補充片語

❶ get something ready 將～準備好

例 **Please get your documents ready.**（請將您的文件準備好。）

解 一般我們說「將…準備好」使用 **get something ready** 表示。

❷ call up 打電話

例 **Call me up if anything is needed.**（如果你需要甚麼就打給我。）

解 在口語中說到「打電話」這個動作可使用 **call up**，注意若使用代名詞則是 **call someone up**。

In Other Words

❶ Do you have these documents in English with you? =Have you had these documents in English with you（請問有準備好這些英文版的文件在身上嗎？）

解 雖說用 **do** 開頭表示現在式，**have** 開頭表示過去完成式，但在口語中也常習慣（尤其英式英語系國家）使用 **have** 開頭詢問，此時表示更加著重在「是否已經準備好」這件事情上。

❷ There is no affidavit from the parents. = The affidavit from the parents is missing.（少了爸媽同意小朋友出國的宣誓證明。）

解 在情境中，要表示「我要找一個東西但沒看到」，要表現「沒有～（東西）」的時候，除了簡單的 These is no ～以外，英文常會使用 missing（缺掉的；找不到的）。Something is missing 就是「什麼東西不見了」、「缺了什麼東西」的意思。

地勤工作解說

一般而言，年滿六歲至未滿 12 歲以下單獨旅行的兒童，必須向航空公司申請「未成年者獨自搭機」的服務，並依照行程航段繳付相關費用。而上述情境，由於南非政府特別針對 18 歲以下兒童及青少年出入境或過境於南非，依不同狀況乘客須備妥相關英文文件。

前輩經驗巧巧說

上述有關飛往或過境南非無父母陪同之未成年孩童，就算有其他親屬或 18 歲以上成人陪同，仍須提出相關文件，否則在南非可能會被海關懷疑這位未成年孩童及同行者之間的關係。此最新規定之訂定是由於近年日益嚴重的拐賣兒童，已經成為非洲乃至全世界的問題，常有販賣兒童、青少年的人口販子，從非洲其他國家出口未成年孩童，將南非當作據點，強迫賣淫或是奴役他們。

身為地勤常常會遇到哪個國家又改了規定，或是多了什麼規定，通常這些變更都會從總公司發出訊息，告訴各航站主管，督導會在 briefing 時提醒大家，並且將訊息公佈在佈告欄上。所以大家要常留意佈告欄上，是不是有新的國際規定。此外，最好也能了解規定背後的原因，如上述的南非，畢竟多了規定對乘客都會造成不方便，若乘客有所抱怨，也可能告知其原因，讓乘客較能理解，怨氣會降低一些喔。

1-23 落地簽

情境介紹

一位旅客和五歲小孩出發前往南京，但旅客沒有台胞證需到當地辦落地簽。

情境對話

Track 23

C ▸ Claire，Y ▸ Mr. Yang

Y: We are going to Nanjing.

C: Ok, may I have your passports, please?

Y: Ok, can we sit together? I have to take care of my son.

C: Sure, today this flight is not fully booked and we will arrange your seats together.

Y: That's great.

C: Would you prefer the seats close to a window or aisle?

Y: What is the seating configuration of this flight?

C: There are three seats in a row of this aircraft.

Y: Ok, I see. Then we choose seats closed to a window.

C: No problem. Your seats are 25A and 25B. These two seats are in front of this airplane.

Y: Thank you.

C: Sir, could I have your Mainland travel permits?

Y: Do you mean Tai-Bao-Zheng?

C: Yes.

Y: Oh, we don't have that, but we would like to apply landing visa in Nanjing airport.

C: I see. May I see your Taiwan ID card and your son's Taiwan Resident book?

Y: Sure.

C: Do you have photos with you?

Y: No, is it possible to take photos in Nanjing airport?

C: Yes, there is a photograph facility in Nanjing airport. Let me remind you that the visa on arrival is only for single entry to China. If you go to China next time, you need to apply new Mainland Travel permit.

Y: I understand, thank you.

譯文

Y: 我們要去南京。

C: 好的，麻煩您們的護照。

Y: 請問我們可以坐一起嗎？我必須照顧我兒子。

C: 當然沒問題，今天班機不滿我們將幫您把位置安排在一起。

Y: 太好了。

C: 請問比較喜歡靠窗還是走道的位置？

Y: 請問這班飛機的座位配置是什麼樣的？

C: 一排有三個位置。

Y: 好的，那我們選靠窗戶的。

C: 沒問題，你們的位置 25A 和 25B 是屬於前排座位。

Y: 謝謝你。

C: 先生，我可以跟你借一下入境大陸的許可證嗎？

Y: 你説的是台胞證嗎？

C: 是的。

Y: 喔，我們沒有台胞證，但我要在南京機場申請落地簽。

C: 好的，我明白了。那我可以看一下你們的台灣身分證，還有你兒子的戶籍謄本嗎？

Y: 當然。

C: 你身上有帶照片嗎？

Y: 沒有，我們可以在南京機場拍嗎？

C: 可以，南京機場有照相設備。提醒您落地簽只能一次性的進入大陸。如果您下次還要去中國，您需要申請新的台胞證喔。

Y: 我了解，謝謝。

英文母語者這麼說

你有帶照片在身上嗎？

中式英文：Do you have your photo on you?

正確說法：Do you have photos with you?

on 是指物品放在…之上，但此句並不是真的指放照片在你身上，而是要問有沒有照片，用 with you 比較恰當。

字彙解析

- **arrange** *v.* 安排

  John arranges accommodations for our trip.（約翰替我們的旅行安排了住宿。）

- **configuration** *n.* 結構；表面配置

  What is the seating configuration of this train?（這火車的座位配置是怎樣的？）

- **row** *n.* 排；行

  Hank always sits in the first row of the class.（Hank 在課堂上總是喜歡坐在第一排。）

- **permit** *n.* 許可證；執照

  We lost our entry permits of this conference.（我們弄丟了這場研討會的通行許可證。）

- **apply** *v.* 申請

  Please remember to apply eletronic visa before going to Australia.（去澳洲之前請記得申請電子簽證。）

- **photograph** *n.* 照片

  Most girls like to take many photographs when traveling.（大部份女生在旅行時喜歡拍很多的照片。）

- **facility** *v.* 設施；設備

  Benson would like to rent a suite with a cooking facility.（Benson 想租附有廚房設備的套房。）

補充片語

❶ take care of 照顧；留意

例 Please take care of children safety when taking escalator.（搭乘手扶梯時請留意小孩子的安全。）

❷ close to 靠近；接近於

例 Jane lives closed to the department store.（Jane 住在靠近百貨公司的地方。）

In Other Words

❶ May I see your Taiwan ID card and your son's Taiwan Resident book? = Could you please present your Taiwan ID card and your son's Taiwan Resident Book to me?

解 may I see「我可以看」是以櫃台員工本身為主詞來查看客人所帶的證件，我們也可將主詞換為是客人，請求旅客出示文件，因此也可說「Could you please present 可以請您出示」，此種說法也不失禮貌。

地勤工作解說

某些國家可以讓旅客到當地辦理落地簽，地勤必須注意旅客所持的證件是符合該國家的規定，例如護照效期至少要有六個月或是需備有照片和其他證明文件等。此篇對話中為例，目的地國家為中國，台灣旅客前往中國須持有護照以及台胞證。如旅客沒有台胞證或是台胞證過期，可以至當地城市申請落地簽，但必須備有有效期的護照以及台灣身分證；然而在台灣 14 歲以下的孩童尚未有台灣身分證，因此未滿 14 歲的孩童可用戶籍謄本或戶口名簿去申請台胞證落地簽。

前輩經驗巧巧說

近幾年，有越來越多的國家開放給台灣旅客能免簽證前往該地遊玩。一般民眾會誤以為對於所有免簽證國家只需持有護照即可前往，然而有些國家並非是完全免簽證，而是指旅客持有有效期限內的護照或相關證件至當地辦理落地簽，或是出發前至該國家移民署網站辦理網上簽證。例如台灣旅客去香港，除了護照外，必須持有效期台胞證或是先到香港移民署網站先申請港簽並將港簽列印下來，旅客是不能到香港當地才上網申請簽證的。持有台灣護照的旅客前往泰國，可以到泰國機場辦理落地簽，但必須注意護照效期需滿六個月以上，如效期少於六個月則無法申請。另外，台灣籍旅客前往美國觀光，出發前得先上美國官方網站申請電子簽證 ESTA，也是無法到美國當地才申請簽證。因此劃位櫃檯人員必須注意旅客們所持的證件是否符合各國的簽證或落地簽規定，以免旅客因證件不符而被遣返回來。

1-24 奧客：行李超重

情境介紹

一位打扮亮麗的女士要搭機到巴西聖保羅，有一件行李超重但不願意支付超重費用。

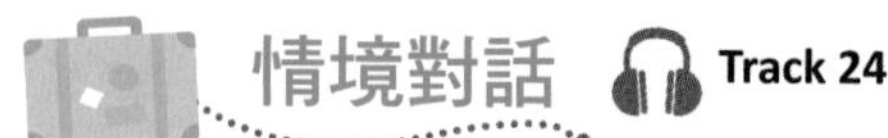

情境對話 Track 24

I ▸ Ian，M ▸ Madam，S ▸ Supervisor

I: I'm sorry, Madam, this piece is overweight. It's 28 kg.

M: But we can have four pieces, right? Just share the weight to another one.

I: Sorry, Madam, the rule is each baggage needs to be less than 20kg, even if there is extra 3kg airport waiver, the baggage is still 5kg overweight. And the other three baggage have all reached the limit as well.

M: Okay, so what now?

I: You can discard some things to reduce the weight, or you will be charged for extra fee.

M: How much is it?

I: It'll be 100 US Dollars.

M: What!? Only 5kg? We usually took business class! How can you charge that much from a frequent customer?

I: I'm sorry, Madams, you can repack your baggage to make it under 23kg, then you'll not be charged.

M: No! It's ridiculous! I want to talk to your manager.

S: How can I help you?

M: I don't want to waste my time, just tell me why I should pay 100 US Dollars for that 5 kg?

S: I'm sorry, Madam. According to the tickets, your baggage allowance is four pieces, 23kg each.

M: We used to take a business class! Don't you have any discount for frequent customers!?

S: Sorry. If you would like to have extra baggage allowance, you're welcome to join our frequent flyer membership and earn the mileage. When you earn over 30,000 miles, you become our silver card member, which could have extra baggage allowance.

M: Oh, all right.

譯文

I: 嗯…太太，這件超重了，它有 28 公斤。

M: 但我們可以拿 4 件行李不是嗎？你就把重量分到其他件去啊。

I: 不好意思，太太，規定是每一件行李要在 20 公斤以下，就算在機場我們會多給 3 公斤的重量免除額，這件還是超過 5 公斤。而且您另外 3 件也都已經達到重量的上限了。

M: 是喔，那現在要怎麼辦？

I: 你可以拿掉一些東西減少重量，不然就要付超重費用。

M: 那是多少錢？

I: 要 100 美金。

M: 什麼！？才 5 公斤耶！我們通常都搭商務艙的耶！你們怎麼可以跟常客收那麼多錢啊？

I: 抱歉，太太，您可以重新打包你的行李讓它降到 23 公斤以下，這樣的話就不用被收費了。

M: 不要！這太扯了吧！叫你們經理出來。

S: 早安，太太。我能幫您什麼？

M: 好啦，我不想浪費時間，請你告訴我為什麼才超重 5 公斤就要我付 100 塊美金？

S: 不好意思，太太，讓我解釋給您聽。根據您這次買的機票，您的行李限額是 4 件行李，每件 23 公斤。

M: 我們以往都是搭商務艙的！你們沒有任何優惠給常客嗎！？

S: 抱歉，沒有喔，如果您們想要更多的行李額度，歡迎您們加入我們的飛行常客會員累積里程數。當您累積超過 30000 哩，您就成為我們的銀卡會員，就可以擁有更多的行李額度。

M: 喔，好吧！

英文母語者這麼說

The baggage is still 5 kg overweight.

（這件行李還是超過 5 公斤。）

非 The baggage is still overweight 5kg. 這裏 overweight 的用法要特別注意，在中文裡我們會把「超過」放在「5 公斤」的前面，但是在英文裡面，會先說「5 公斤」再說「超過了」，如同「我哥哥大我 2 歲」，英文是 "My brother is 2 years older than me." 也是先說「2 歲」，再說「比我大」，這是英文文法上與中文不同的地方，請大家留意。

You are welcome to join our frequent flyer membership and earn the mileage.（歡迎您們加入我們的飛行常客會員累積里程數。）

非 We are welcome to join our frequent flyer membership and earn the mileage. 在中文裡「歡迎您」是「我們」歡迎「您」的加入，但在上述句子裡要注意的是 welcome 的用法，它是屬於形容詞或是動詞呢？

例句的用法是形容詞的用法，形容「您」，「您是受歡迎的」對於「加入我們的飛行常客會員」，所以是 You are welcome（您是受歡迎的）to（對於）join our frequent flyer membership。

字彙解析

- **trunk** *n.* 大行李箱

  Whose trunk is that?（那是誰的大行李箱？）

- **airport waiver** *n.* 機場免除額（行李重量）

  Usually, there is 3kg airport waive to each passenger of economy class.（通常每一位經濟艙旅客享有 3 公斤行李的機場免除重量額度。）

- **overweight** *adj.* 超重的

  The vet told me my cat is overweight.（獸醫跟我說我的貓超重了。）

- **reach** *v.* 達到

  He reached the goal in last minute.（他在最後一分鐘抵達終點。）

- **frequent customer** *n.* 常客

  Our frequent customers could have extra 10% off during our anniversary sale.（我們的常客在週年慶拍賣可以享有九折的優惠。）

- **ridiculous** *adj.* 可笑的，荒謬的

  It is very ridiculous that educators accept bribery.（那些教育者接受賄賂真是可笑。）

- **baggage allowance** *n.* 行李限額

  Your baggage allowance depends on the tickets you buy.（你的行李限額依照你買的票會有所不同。）

補充片語

❶ as well 也

例 I will go to Tokyo next month as well.（我下個月也要去東京。）

解 as well 就是「也」的意思，用法與 too 相似，都是放在句尾。若能習慣並熟練的使用 as well 取代更多人熟知的 too，會讓人有「你是慣用英語的人」的錯覺喔！

In Other Words

❶ How can I help you? = May I help you?

解 這兩句都是相當有禮貌的問法，詢問「請問我可以幫您什麼忙嗎？」，也可以使用 Can I help you，但用 may 開頭會比 can 來得更尊敬。因此在機場或是飯店，通常還是使用 May I help you?

地勤工作解說

「行李」常常是旅客最常發生問題的一個項目，因為在各航空公司有不同規定，且有些國家亦有特別的行李規定，而乘客買了不同艙等或飛往不同國家的機票也有不一樣的行李限制。一般機票給予的行李限額分成「重量限制」與「件數限制」。飛往美洲國家的機票較常用給予「件數限制」，而其他地區則較常以「重量限制」作為行李限額。但也不是絕對的，所以在辦理登機手續時一定要看清楚乘客的機票怎麼寫喔。

前輩經驗巧巧說

有些東西只能放手提不能放託運，有些東西只能託運不能手提，有些尺寸過長，有些太重要另外處理…各式各樣的狀況都可能會出現在櫃台。（筆者目前遇過最妙的是觀賞用的魚，用塑膠袋連水包在塑膠袋，再放進保麗龍箱裏，當時很訝異這樣竟然可以托運！）

關於行李限額是以「件數」或是「重量」計算，通常美洲線是以「件數」計算，經濟艙是 2 件 23 公斤以下為限，其他地區通常是以重量計算，每位乘客可以攜帶 20 公斤的行李，幾件都沒關係，加起來不超過 20 公斤即可。但筆者就有遇到特殊的案例，客人飛往德國，托運兩件行李總共 23 公斤，以為歐洲都是重量制，判斷客人沒超重，當時也沒再次確認機票上的行李限額，但由於此客人的長程段是搭乘歐洲的航空公司，行李限額為一件不超過 23 公斤，導致旅客後來被酌收超件費且產生客訴！通常奧客的抱怨都很長，礙於版面已縮編至最簡化，千萬不要覺得這麼輕易就可以打發掉喔。

1-25 乘客將證件放在托運行李

情境介紹

一位學生要前往杜拜當交換學生，不小心將學校給的文件放在託運行李裡面，check in 之後才想起來要放在隨身行李。地勤人員帶領學生到海關，請海關人員將已經過關的行李取回，拿出文件後再次託運行李。

情境對話 Track 25

S ▸ Student，C ▸ Cathy

S: I'm going to Dubai.

C: Your passport and visa, please.

(Hand in passport and visa)

C: Can you find me in which page your visa is?

S: Oh! Okay!

C: Any baggage to check in?

S: Yes, two pieces.

C: No problem. Here are your baggage receipts and boarding pass. Thank you!

(10 mins later)

S: Excuse me.

C: Hi. Anything I can help?

S: I am sorry. I have my school letter in my check in luggage. Can you help me to retrieve it?

C: Oh. The luggage has already gone through the customs. Do you know which one?

S: It's mine, the big yellow case.

C: Can I have your baggage receipt?

S: Here.

C: Okay. I will pass the baggage receipt number to our staffs in cargo department. They will help us to find it. Now, please come with me.

S: Where are we going?

C: All luggage sending to cargo department for loading up need to be checked by the customs. Since it has passed the customs, we are not able to retrieve it by ourselves for fear that someone sneaking stuffs something in it. So we are going to collect it from the customs downstairs.

S: Wow. I have no idea. I'm sorry for bothering you.

C: No problem. We had better hurry up. The flight will be closed in 10 minutes. Checking in again takes time, too.

譯文

S: 我要去杜拜。

C: 麻煩您的護照和簽證。

（遞護照和簽證。）

C: 可以請你幫我找一下你的簽證在哪一頁嗎？

S: 噢，好。

C: 有要託運的行李嗎？

S: 有，兩件。

C: 沒問題，這裡是您的行李收據和登機證。謝謝。

（十分鐘後）

S: 不好意思。

C: 噢，嗨。需要我幫忙嗎？

S: 不好意思，我把我的錄取信放在托運行李了。你可以幫我追回來嗎？

C: 噢。行李已經到海關去了耶。你知道是哪一個行李嗎？

S: 是我的，大的黃色的箱子。

C: 可以給我你的行李收據嗎？

S: 在這裏。

C: 好的。我會將行李收據號碼交給我們貨運部同事，他們會幫忙找到它。現在要請你們跟我來。

S: 我們要去哪？

C: 所有的行李在送到貨運部門準備上飛機前，都要經過海關檢查。既然它已經過海關了，我們就無法自己追回來，因為怕有人會偷偷塞東西進去。所以我們要去樓下海關那裡把行李追回來。

S: 哇。我都不知道。這麼打擾你真是不好意思。

C: 沒關係。我們最好快一點，因為飛機再 10 分鐘就要關了。要再次托運也是要花時間的。

英文母語者這麼說

Can you find me in which page your visa is?（可以幫我找到你的簽證在哪一頁嗎？）

不要說 Can you find me which page your visa is in 也不要說 Can you find me which page is your visa in。先說前者，in 是和 which page 在一起的，小心不要把他們分開了；後者要注意子句如果是問句，動詞的位置要回到直述句的位置。

All luggage sent to cargo department for loading up needs to be checked by the customs.（所有送到貨運部準備裝載的行李都要經海關檢查。）

不要說 All luggage sent to cargo department prepare / ready for loading up need to be checked by the customs。這句話裡面「準備」在英文裡如果加上去會變得多餘，因此不需要說出來。

字彙解析

- **retrieve** *v.* 重新得到、取回；挽回、救回

  It takes time to retrieve the data.（救回那些資料需要花些時間。）

- **downstairs** *adj.* 樓下的

  He is downstairs.（他在樓下。）

補充片語

❶ load up 裝載（貨物）

例 They finished loading up in only 30 minutes.

（他們只花了 30 分鐘就完成裝貨。）

解 若在貨運部工作，常會使用到跟貨物有關的詞，load up 是專指「把解：貨裝上貨艙」這個動作。

In Other Words

❶ Can you find me in which page your visa is? = Can you find the page of your visa for me?（可以幫我找到你們簽證所在的那一頁嗎？）

❷ I will pass the baggage receipt number to our staffs in cargo department; they will help us to find it. = I will let my colleagues in cargo department know the receipt number of the baggage; they will help us to find it.（我會將行李收據的號碼告訴貨運部的同事，他們會幫忙把它找出來。）

地勤工作解說

在機場也會遇到客人將重要的證件、文件放在託運行李裡 check in 之後，到了登機口了才發現。這時又要匆匆忙忙再跑回櫃檯，請地勤人員協助將行李取回，拿到文件後，再次 check in 行李。這樣就會多花很多時間。若時間充裕還好，要是時間已經不早的話就會非常趕！

前輩經驗巧巧說

這也是一篇真實案例，讓我印象深刻。學生要到杜拜，行李已經 check in 後，要再次調整行李，但前面的行李已經過了 X 光機準備上貨艙了。只好帶著他們先請海關人關將行李取出，一般人是不能隨便進去海關的，只能在外面等候。行李調整後，要重新 check in、檢查行李。有時候若行李已經上了飛機才要取回，那就得從機邊下行李，由機邊督導提到登機門，然後再從機邊把行李送上飛機，不論哪一種方式都會花費很多時間。

Part 2 出境

2-1 貴賓室 Lounge

情境介紹

一位商務艙客人到貴賓室，臨時需要收一件傳真資料。

情境對話 Track 26

S ▸ Stacy，B ▸ Mr. Black

S: Good evening, sir. May I have your lounge invitation?

B: Here you go.

S: Thank you. Please enjoy it.

B: Do you have anything warm, such as soup, noodles or else?

S: Yes. We offer three kinds of soup today, including Taiwanese fish soup, Japanese miso soup with tofu, and Mushroom cream soup. We also provide Taiwanese noodles and two flavors of pasta. You can order your meal after settling down. There is a menu on each table.Our staffs will serve you when entering the lounge.

(15 minutes later)

B: Excuse me.

S: Yes, Sir. How can I help you?

B: I just got an email and need to receive a fax from my office. Do you have a fax machine here?

S: Yes. Here is our fax number, and the country code is +886.

B: Okay. Thank you very much. I am sending the fax number to my secretary now.

(3 minutes later)

S: Oh, there is a fax coming in.

B: Great. It's faster than I thought.

S: Here. Is it what you are waiting for?

B: Um... yes, it is exactly what I need now. Thank you.

S: No problem.

B: By the way, I'm taking ZZ234 to London, would you remind me to board the flight? I might be too concentrated on my work to miss the flight.

S: Certainly. We will announce then. Please don't worry.

譯文

S: 晚安，先生。可以給我您的貴賓室邀請函嗎？

B: 在這。

S: 謝謝。請進。

B: 請問你們有沒有一點溫熱的東西，像是湯啊、麵啊或其他之類的東西？

S: 有。我們今天提供三種湯品，有台灣風味魚湯、日本風的豆腐味噌湯，及蘑菇濃湯。我們也提供台灣陽春麵及兩種口味的義大利麵。您可以在安頓好之後點餐。每個座位上都有一份菜單。您進門後我們的工作人員就會為您服務。

（15 分鐘後）

B: 抱歉打擾一下。

S: 是，先生。有什麼需要幫忙嗎？

B: 我剛收到一封 email，需要收一件我辦公室傳來的傳真。你們這裡有傳真機嗎？

S: 有。這是我們的傳真號碼，國碼是+886。

B: 好。非常感謝你。我現在傳傳真號碼給我的秘書。

（3 分鐘後）

S: 噢，有傳真進來了。

B: 太好了。比我想像中快。

S: 這裡。這是您在等的資料嗎？

B: 嗯…對，這就是我現在需要的。非常謝謝你。

S: 不客氣。

B: 對了，我搭 ZZ234 班機到倫敦，你們可以提醒我登機嗎？我可能會太專注於工作而錯過班機。

S: 當然。到時候我們會廣播。請不用擔心。

英文母語者這麼說

Excuse me.（抱歉打擾一下。）

> 雖然這是很基本的句子，但若太緊張還是有人會用 *I'm sorry* 開頭的喔。

Our staffs will serve you when entering the lounge.（您進門後我們的工作人員就會為您服務。）

> 請注意 when 作為「當…的時候」後面要接動名詞，不然就是整個子句。有時候不小心會混淆變成 *our staffs will serve you when you entering the lounge.* 要特別留意。

字彙解析

- **lounge** *n.* 貴賓室

  You can go to the lounge to take a rest.（您可以到貴賓室休息一下。）

- **invitation** *n.* 邀請函

  You need an invitation to go to VIP night.（你需要邀請函才能去

VIP 之夜。）

- **tofu** *n.* 豆腐

He likes tofu very much.（他非常喜歡豆腐。）

- **flavor** *n.* 口味

Which flavor would you like?（你喜歡哪一種口味？）

- **concentrated** *adj.* 專心的

He is very concentrated when driving.（他開車時非常專心。）

補充片語

❶ wait for 等待

例 I am waiting for an important phone call.（我在等一通重要的電話。）

解 wait 本身可以接名詞，但習慣上有些句子的用法還是會加上 for。

In Other Words

❶ Our staffs will serve you when entering the lounge. = Our staffs will serve you when you enter the lounge.（您進門後我們的工作人員就會為您服務。）

解 when 作為「當…的時候」後面要接動名詞，因此在這裡用 you enter the lounge 取代 entering the lounge。

地勤工作解說

貴賓室僅提供給商務艙客人及累積足夠里程數的常客使用。若你搭乘商務艙，你在櫃檯辦理登機時，登機證會附有一張貴賓室邀請函。另外還有一種貴賓室，是由信用卡公司所提供的，但這一類型的貴賓室有時還是得要付費才能使用。

前輩經驗巧巧說

貴賓室也是航空公司搶客人的一個戰場。如同前面所提過的，航空公司最希望爭取的就是頂級的客人，因此在貴賓室這一塊，當然要好好經營。不過，也因各機場規模不一樣，有些機場能提供的貴賓室品質可能還是有限。但也有不少航空公司會大手筆的翻修貴賓室，就是為了提供頂級客人們最棒的服務。有興趣的朋友可以上網搜尋各航空公司於各機場的貴賓室，某些航空甚至還有頭等艙貴賓才能使用的專用「航廈」呢。

2-2 Boarding Gate 候機室

情境介紹

地勤人員於登機前提早抵達候機室，執行登機前的相關作業。一位乘客提太多手提行李，引起地勤人員注意。

情境對話 Track 27

J ▸ Joanna，R ▸ Rita，M ▸ Mike

(Joanna and Rita are at the boarding gate. Joanna takes charge of the boarding gate)

J: Rita, please walk around the waiting room and be aware of the carry-on baggage which are oversized or, sometimes too many pieces. Please be back here for boarding 20 minutes later.

R: No problem.

(In front of the perfume shopping corner, a man with 2 big shopping bags and one huge backpack and a suitcase moving haltingly towards the boarding gate)

R: Excuse me, sir. Are you travelling alone?

M: Oh, yes.

R: Are these all your luggage?

M: Yes, they are all mine. I bought some cigarette and cosmetics at a duty free store inside the airport.

R: I'm sorry, sir. You have too many pieces of carry-on baggage. We need to check in at least 2 pieces of them. May I have your passport and boarding pass please?

M: But they are purchased inside the airport.

R: Sorry, sir. No matter where you bought them, they are all so-called "carry-on baggage".

M: Okay.

R: Please come with me. Do you have check-in luggage already?

M: Yes... a lot.

R: I'm afraid you might need to pay for your shopping booty.

M: No way.

譯文

（Joanna、Rita 在登機門。Joanna 負責管理登機門作業。）

J: Rita，請你在候機室這裡繞一繞，注意一下過大的登機行李，或是有時候太多件登機行李的。請在 20 分鐘後回到這裡處理登機。

R: 沒問題。

（在賣香水處前面，一位男士帶著兩個大購物袋、一個巨大的背包以及一個登機箱，步履蹣跚地往登機門移動）

R: 不好意思，先生。您今天一個人旅行嗎？

M: 喔，對。

R: 這些全部都是您的行李嗎？

M: 對，都是我的。我在機場免稅店買了些香煙和化妝品。

R: 抱歉，先生。你帶太多登機行李了。我們至少得要托運其中兩件行李。可以給我您的護照及登機證嗎？

M: 可是這些都是在機場裡買的耶。

R: 抱歉，先生。不論您是在哪裡買的，他們都是所謂的「登機行李」。

M: 好吧。

R: 請跟我走。您已經有托運的行李了嗎？

M: 是啊…很多。

R: 您恐怕要為您血拼的戰利品付錢了。

M: 不會吧。

英文母語者這麼說

Please be back here for boarding 20 minutes later.

（請於 20 分鐘後回到這裡進行登機。）

請不要說成 *Please 20 minutes later come back here for boarding*
請記得，英文中的時間副詞要放在句子的最後面。

字彙解析

- **perfume** *n.* 香水
  I have some collection of perfume.（我有一些香水的收藏。）

- **haltingly** *adv.* 蹣跚地
  He walks haltingly after falling down from the steps last week.（他上禮拜從台階上摔下來後，走路走得很蹣跚。）

- **cigarette** *n.* 香菸
  This is my favorite brand of cigarette.（這是我最喜歡的香煙品牌。）

- **purchase** *v.* 購買
  The sculpture was purchased by a financial business group.（這雕像被一個金融集團買下了。）

- **booty** *n.* 戰利品
  My sister shows her shopping booty of Tokyo on her Facebook.（我姊在她的臉書上秀出她在東京的血拼戰利品。）

補充片語

❶ walk around 隨意走走；繞著…走

例 My cat likes to walk around the neighborhood.（我的貓喜歡在住家附近隨意走走。）

❷ no matter 不論、不管

例 No matter how tired you are, the work must be done today.（不管你多累，這工作今天要做完。）

In Other Words

❶ No matter where you bought them, they are all so-called"carry-on baggages". = Regardless of the place you bought them, they are all so-called"carry-on baggages".（不論您在哪裡購買的，他們都是所謂的「登機行李」。）

解 這裡使用 regardsless of～取代了 no matter～，請留意 regardless of 需接名詞，這裡是用 the place you bought them 取代了 where you bought them（但是原本的 where 也是可以作為名詞接續的喔）。

地勤工作解說

身為一個地勤人員，在登機前有很多工作要做。為了每位乘客的安全，於候機室再次檢查登機行李是必要的。如有乘客攜帶太多登機行李而被要求託運，先查看他／她的行李紀錄，確認他／她還在行李限額內。否則的話，他／她就要付超重費用，這是很花時間的（有時地勤人員要為了這付款動作奔波於 information 櫃台與登機門之間）。再者，就如我們之前提過的，如果有嬰兒車在該班機，要確保於登機前將之收起來，以於機邊上載，這也需要時間。

前輩經驗巧巧說

當乘客完成登機手續後，經過海關，抵達候機室，對地勤人員而言則是更加分秒必爭了。如上述所提，在候機室要再次檢查客人們的登機行李，為了飛行安全及其他乘客的權益，過多、過重的行李都要要求託運。所謂的「登機行李」包含了在機場免稅店購買的商品，文中的男士就是在免稅店買了太多東西，引起地勤人員注意，而要求託運。筆者曾經遇過比較誇張的是一位外籍勞工朋友，工作結束要搬回家鄉，似乎覺得臺灣的洗衣精很好用，塞了大概 8 包補充包在登機行李（很重！），但在辦理登機時由友人保管沒有告知地勤人員，到候機室被其他地勤人員發現她小小一個登機箱怎麼拖得這麼辛苦，才在登機門處的磅秤上秤重發現。這要是從頭上的置物櫃掉下來可不得了啊…也因此，這位外籍朋友繳了超重費用。有時因為登機門無法進行收費（含刷卡、開收據等作業），時間如果又很趕了，地勤在這時就要衝刺於櫃台與登機門之間了…另外還有其他相關的例外狀況，將在接下來的篇章分享。

2-3 登機通告

情境介紹

Speedy 航空公司 S702 9:00am 前往大阪的航班，登機前的廣播。

情境對話 Track 28

Good morning ladies and gentlemen, Speedy Flight S702 to Osaka will soon be ready for general boarding in 10 mins, please remain seated.

We would like to invite passengers with disabilities or traveling with infants and passengers requiring assistance to come forward for priority boarding.

In the meantime, we would like to extend a warm welcome to our First and Business Class passengers and Speedy Club members, invite you to board with priority.

Would all remaining passengers please have your boarding passes ready, and we will soon make another boarding announcement. Thank You !

For your safety and comfort on board, the allowance of your carry-on baggage is within one piece with 7 kilograms. If you carry over-piece or over-weight hand baggage, please kindly contact our staffs and we will check-in your bag at the boarding gate. Thank you for your patience and cooperation!

各位旅客您好：
速達航空公司 702 往大阪即將於 10 分鐘後開始登機，請先留在原位。
我們將優先邀請需要特別照顧以及行動不便或與嬰兒同行的旅客先行登機.
同時，我們誠摯歡迎頭等客艙、商務客艙、速達會員於開始登機時優先登機。
其他旅客請您留在原座並準備好登機證，稍後我們將再做登機廣播！
另外，為了各位旅客於機上的安全及舒適，本航班的手提行李限重 7 公斤一件，若您攜帶超過一件手提行李、或超重的手提行李，請與登機門地勤人員聯繫，我們將替您安排行李託運。
謝謝您的耐心與配合！

英文母語者這麼說

（我們將優先邀請需要特別照顧行動不便或與嬰兒同行的旅客先行登機。）

中式英文：We invite passengers with disabilities and need care for and traveling with infants to come first for boarding.

正確說法：We would like to invite passengers with disabilities or traveling with infants and passengers requiring assistance to come forward for priority boarding.

照顧的英文雖然是 care for，但上述中式英文表達會變成「我們邀請照顧旅客的人」句意表達完全錯誤，此句要描述的是需求協助的旅客是特別需要照顧的，因此正確說法為 passengers requiring assistance。先行登機不要說 come first ，這樣太過口語化，應用 come forward 比較正式，且如要強調『優先』可用 priority 來表達。

- **remain** *v.* 保持；留待

This villa remains clean because the housekeeper cleans it twice a week.（這棟別墅保持得很乾淨因為房子主人一星期打掃兩次。）

- **disability** *n.* 行動不便；殘障

We will arrange the front seat for disability passenger.（我們會安排前面的位置給行動不便的旅客。）

- **priority** *n.* 優先；優先考慮的事

Safety is top priority for each airline.（安全是每一家航空公司優先考慮的事。）

- **extend** *v.* 致；提供；給予

All staffs in this hotel extend a warm welcome to every visitor.（這家飯店的全體員工熱烈的歡迎每位旅客。）

- **comfort** *v.* 安逸；舒適

We enjoy the comfort of this hotel.（我們享受著這家飯店的舒適。）

- **contact** *v.* 與…聯絡；交涉

When you arrive in Paris, please contact with the local tour leader.（當你到巴黎時，請與當地的導遊聯絡。）

- **patience** *n.* 耐心

Nurses require patience for taking care of patients.（護士需要有耐心照顧病患。）

補充片語

❶ come forward 向前

例 Plesae come forward when the teacher calls your name.
（當老師叫到你名字時，請走向前來。）

❷ In the meantime 同時；在那當時

例 In the meantime, the fireman puts out the fire and rescues a girl.
（同時消防員撲滅了火也救了一位女孩。）

In Other Words

❶ For your safety and comfort on board, the allowance of your carry-on baggage is within one piece with 7 kilograms.＝The hand carry luggage of each passenger is within one piece under 7 kilograms for the safety and comfort.（為了各位旅客於機上的安全及舒適，本航班的手提行李限重 7 公斤一件。）

解 換句話說，可省略 **allowance** 此字，直接簡單明瞭點出手提行李限額是多少，也可避免廣播詞饒口。另外，**with** 也可用 **under** 來代替。

地勤工作解說

航班登機之前，登機門的地勤會先做說明登機順序的廣播，以避免造成登機時的擁擠。登機順序會先以特別需要照顧或行動不便的旅客為第一優先，例如有輪椅旅客和行動不便的年長者，以及嬰幼兒隨行的旅客也可優先登機，以免讓這些旅客久候排隊。另外，地勤人員須留意乘客們的手提行李重量與尺寸必須在規定範圍內，這是為了預防當飛行途中遇到不穩定的氣流時，導致上層置物箱的行李掉落而砸傷乘客。因此，在登機之前也會先廣播手提行李的規定。

前輩經驗巧巧說

地勤人員在念廣播詞時必須逐字清楚並且速度要放慢，這樣才能確保旅客們清楚聽到廣播內容。另外，在登機之前工作人員在登機門附近加以巡視，如發現有需要協助的旅客，立即給予適時幫忙。而如有發現行為不當的旅客，如喝醉酒的乘客，必須觀察旅客的意識狀態，避免影響其他人的安全與舒適。因為曾經發生過，有位全身酒味的旅客，上飛機後對空服員以及其他乘客做出不雅的動作，機長到最後決定拒載此位乘客，以避免影響航班運作。此外，手提行李的限額是相當重要的航安之一，也是有真實案例發生，有名婦人帶了一件重達 15 公斤的手提行李上機，在飛行途中因遇到亂流，使得行李滑落而砸傷另一名乘客造成腦震盪。因此登機之前，地勤人員需特別把關留意，預防影響航空安全的事件發生。

2-4 登機證遺失

情境介紹

一位乘客遺失了他的登機證，請地勤人員協助。

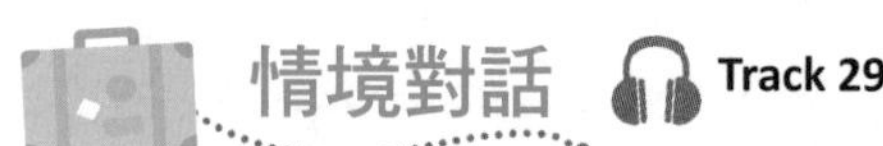

情境對話 Track 29

E ▸ Elena，J ▸ Joanna，W ▸ Mr. Wang

E (supervisor): Joanne, is it your turn to take charge of boarding gate today? Y class of FA456 is over booked again, so I upgrade the seat of this lady who travels alone. Please exchange with her old boarding pass before boarding. I think she has passed the immigration.

J: Okay. I'm just ready to go inside. (At boarding gate 23, 10 minutes before boarding)

W: Excuse me, Miss.

J: Yes, sir.

W: I was shopping at the duty free shop but couldn't find my boarding pass. Can you print a new one?

J: Oh, sorry, sir. I am not able to print a boarding pass here. We don't have the printer here. May I have your passport? I can ask my colleague to do so and bring it in later.

W: Thank you. Please hurry up. I need it to pay up.

J: No problem. (by walkie talkie) Elena.

E (by walkie talkie): Yes?

J (by walkie talkie): Please check boarding number 88, passenger Mr. Wang, he lost his boarding pass, would you please print a new one for him?

E (by walkie talkie): Let me see... okay, no problem. Sophie is going to the gate. I will let her to deliver it.

J (by walkie talkie): Thank you.

W: How was it?

J: No problem. My colleague will deliver your new boarding pass in 5 minutes. Please wait a second.

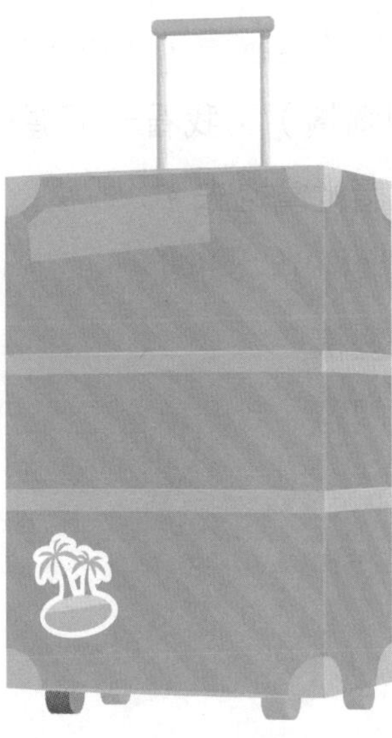

譯文

E （督導）：Joanne，今天輪到你負責管理登機門作業嗎？FA456 經濟艙今天超賣，所以我給這位自己旅行的小姐升等。麻煩你在登機前跟她的舊登機證交換。我想她已經過了移民署了。

J: 好。我準備好要進去了。（3 分鐘後）

W: 不好意思，小姐。

J: 是，先生。

W: 我剛在那邊的免稅店買東西，但找不到我的登機證。你可以幫我印一張新的嗎？

J: 喔，先生抱歉。我這裡沒辦法印登機證。我們這裏沒有印表機。可以給我您的護照嗎？我可以請我同事印然後拿進來。

W: 謝謝。請快一點。我需要它才能付帳單。

J: 好的。（對講機）Elena。

E（對講機）：請說。

J（對講機）：請你看一下登機號碼 88 號，有一位乘客王先生，他遺失了他的登機證，可以請你印一張新的給他嗎？

E（對講機）：我看一下喔…好的，沒問題。Sophie 正要進去登機門。我請她拿過去。

J（對講機）：謝謝。

W: 怎麼樣？

J: 沒問題。我同事會在 5 分鐘內把您的登機證拿進來，請您稍候。

英文母語者這麼說

Is it your turn to take charge of boarding gate today?

（今天輪到你負責管理登機門作業嗎？）

charge 這個字有幾個不同的意思。本句中，是「負責管理」、「掌握」的意思，且一定要與 take 一起出現，不然的話就變成其他意思了。

I'm just ready to go inside.

（我準備好要進去了。）

若從中文去思考這句話的翻譯，很容易會跳出"prepare"這個字，但請留意其實原意是「準備好」而不僅僅是「準備」而已，所以應該使用的是 ready 而不是 prepare。

字彙解析

- **upgrade** *v.* 升等、升級

I paid $100 to upgratde my membership.（我花了 100 元升級我的會員。）

- **exchange** *v.* 交換

He would like to exchange the seat with you.（他想要跟你換座位。）

補充片語

❶ take charge of 負責、管理

例 She takes charge of the branch.（她負責管理這一家分行。）

❷ be able to 能夠、可以

例 You are not able to go to swim today.（你今天不能去游泳。）

❸ pay up 付清（帳款、債務）

例 You must pay up your debt this year.（你今年一定要將債務付清。）

In Other Words

❶ Please exchange with her old boarding pass before boarding. = Please make her old boarding pass to be exchanged.（請跟她的舊登機證交換。）

解 這裡將原本主動式的句子改成被動，中文直譯為「讓她的登機證被交換過來」，本句的動詞是 make，而原本句子中則是以 exchange 當動詞支撐整句話。

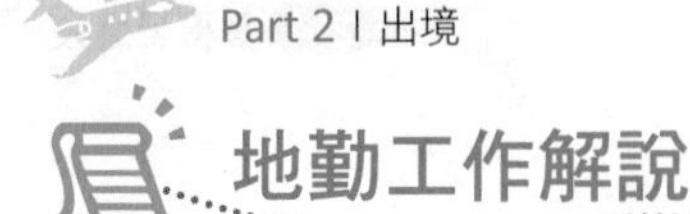

地勤工作解說

如我們之前說過的，有時候班機會被訂滿，或甚至超賣。若可能的話，有些乘客會被升等。但是，有時候升等的人數不足，也就是說地勤人員需要升等更多已經辦完登機手續的客人，所以最後還有誰要被升等會在快要登機的時候決定。這也是為什麼 Elena 要 Joanne 去將舊的登機證換成新的。另一個文中的情形是，乘客遺失了他的登機證。印一張新的登機證是可以的，但極為重要的是要確認該登機證真的遺失了，不然的話，可能會出現兩個人一起來登機，而且是在同一個座位。

前輩經驗巧巧說

當遇到乘客遺失登機證時，還是要請他再次確認全身上下都找過一遍，最好是陪在他身邊看他找，因登機證在這世界上最好僅存在一張，以免出現什麼誤會或奇怪的狀況（比方有人拿著撿到的登機證跑去登機）。另外，若當天有班機超賣，如前面所說過的，若商務艙有座位，可能會將經濟艙客人升等到商務艙，以空出經濟艙的座位。通常當天 briefing 的時候，督導就會告知這一班飛機有多少人要被升等，若辦理登機時有遇到覺得適合升等到商務艙的客人（如單獨旅行、衣著整齊、沒有帶小孩的）就可以立即將他們升等，若人數達到目標，督導也會立即通知櫃台，商務艙已經滿了，不用再轉人上商務艙了。但若到了關櫃台的時候還不足目標人數，督導可能會自行選擇已經辦理登機完的乘客，將他們升等，但因登機證不同，所以要請在登機門的同事將他們的登機證換過來。

2-5 來機延誤

情境介紹

一班由台北出發前往曼谷的航班，原訂 **17:00** 出發，由於來機晚到導致航班延遲起飛，乘客黃太太擔心錯過在曼谷轉機的航班。

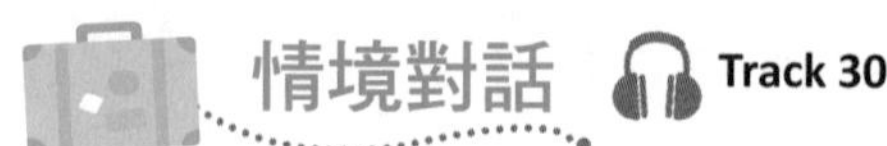

情境對話 Track 30

K ▸ Kevin，H ▸ Mrs. Huang

K: (announcement) Good afternoon, Ladies and gentlemen, Speedy Air regrets to advise you that flight S806 departing for Bangkok has been delayed due to the late arrival of incoming flight, the departure time will be at 18:00. If you require any assistance, please contact our staff at boarding gate 50. We apologize for any inconvenience caused.

H: Hi, I just heard the announcement; this flight will be delayed for one hour. I'm worried about I will miss my connection flight in Bangkok.

K: So sorry, Mrs Huang. Let me see how can I help you. May I see your boarding pass?

H: Ok, here is my boarding pass.

K: Thank you. Let me check your schedule. The departure time of your connection flight in Bangkok is 22:30 and the flight is going to San Francisco, right?

H: Yes, what is the arrival time of S806?

K: The estimated arrival time in Bangkok will be 22:00.

H: I think I'm unable to catch my flight in Bangkok.

K: I think so. Don't worry, Mrs. Huang. I'll help you to rebook your transferred flight to San Francisco. Please wait for a moment.

(3 mins later)

K: Mrs. Huang, I already found the other flight from Bangkok to San Francisco. It's AB230. The departure time in Bangkok is 23:30. You'll have one and half hour to transfer in Bangkok airport. The arrival time in San Francisco is local time 10:00. Is it OK with you?

H: Yes, please change my connection flight to AB230 for me.

譯文

K:（廣播）女士們先生們午安，很抱歉通知您速達航空 S806 前往曼谷的航班由於來機延遲抵達，本航班將延遲起飛，起飛時間將在 18:00。如您需要任何協助，請與我們 50 號登機門地勤人員聯繫。造成您的不便我們深感抱歉。

H: 嗨，我剛剛聽到廣播，這個航班將延遲一個小時才起飛。我擔心將錯過在曼谷的轉機航班。

K: 非常抱歉，黃太太。讓我看看可以怎麼幫您。請給我您的登機證好嗎？

H: 好，這是我的登機證。

K: 謝謝你。我看一下您的行程。您在曼谷的續程航班是前往舊金山起飛時間是 22:30，是嗎？

H: 是的，請問 S806 抵達當地的時間是幾點？

K: 預計抵達曼谷時間為 22:00。

H: 我認為我無法接上在曼谷的航班了。

K: 我也是這麼認為。不要擔心，黃太太，我將幫您重新訂到舊金山的航班。請等我一下。

（3 分鐘後）

K: 黃太太，我已經找到另一班前往舊金山的航班了。這航班在曼谷的起飛時間為 23:30。您在曼谷機場轉機時間將會有一個半小時。抵達舊金山的時間是當地時間 10:00。這樣對您來說可以嗎？

H: 那好，請幫忙將我的轉機航班改為 AB320。

英文母語者這麼說

（由於來機延遲抵達，本航班將延遲起飛。）

中式英文：**Due to the incoming flight is delay, this flight will be delay.**

正確說法：**The flight has been delayed due to the late arrival of incoming flight.**

due to 是「由於、因為」的意思，但英文文法中不能將 due to 放在句首，而是要放在句子的中間。due to 後接名詞。

字彙解析

- **regret** *v.* 為…抱歉；遺憾；懊悔

  Joy regrets to make this decision.（Joy 懊悔做出這個決定。）

- **advise** *v.* 通知；告知

  Please advise us of the exit way if the fire occurred in this building.

  （請告知我們如果這棟大樓發生火災時的逃生路線。）

- **incoming** *adj.* 進來的

  The departure time of this train has been influenced by the incoming train.

  （這班火車的出發時間會被進來的火車而受到影響。）

- **apologize** *v.* 道歉

  Mr. Lin apologizes to him for this car accident.

  （林先生因為這場車禍而向他道歉。）

- **inconvenience** *n.* 不便之處；麻煩

  The elevator out of service caused the convenience.

  （電梯故障造成麻煩。）

- **announcement** *n.* 通告；宣告

  Please make the pre-boarding announcement as soon as possible.（請盡快做登機前的通告。）

補充片語

❶ regret to 為…抱歉；遺憾

例 Manager regrets to make the failure of this case.（經理為此次案子造成的失敗感到抱歉。）

In Other Words

❶ Speedy Air regrets to advise you that flight S806 departing for Bangkok has been delayed due to the late arrival of incoming flight. = Sorry to inform that flight S806 departing for Bangkok has been delayed owing to late arrival of incoming flight.（很抱歉地通知您速達航空 S806 前往曼谷的航班由於來機延遲抵達，本航班將延遲起飛。）

解 regrets to advise 可替換成 sorry to inform 來表示歉意。

❷ I think I am unable to catch my flight in Bangkok. = I cannot take my flight in Bangkok.（我認為無法接上在曼谷的航班了。）

解 可以省略「I think 我認 」，直接說 I cannot 來表達「我無法」。catch 也可用 take 取代，搭飛機的一般說詞 take flight，換句話說的句子更為簡單明瞭。

地勤工作解說

造成航班延誤的原因有很多種，如氣候因素、 機械故障或是來機晚到。其中以「來機晚到」此狀況最常發生。因為每架飛機並不是一天只飛一個航點，尤其是短程線的飛機，通常一天內可能飛三個地方，假如此航班並非為當天此架飛機的第一起站，當然就必須等待來機的抵達。因此第一個起站的航班如延遲出發就會耽誤到下一個站的班機出發時間。

前輩經驗巧巧說

航空公司如確定來機延誤而影響到出發航班的時間，都會在第一時間通知旅客。如在登機門，地勤人員必須廣播航班延遲的原因。通常大部份旅客會有轉機，如果因為航班延誤而導致旅客無法接上續程航班，地勤人員將會協助客人重新改訂轉機的航班，當找到替代航班時，一定要清楚地告知旅客新的續程航班出發時間以及抵達時間，還有中途的轉機時間，詢問旅客是否同意此安排。先前曾發生過，未親自徵求旅客的意願，地勤人員就先改訂了旅客的轉機航班，而造成客人的不悅。因為航班的延誤已經打亂旅客的原訂行程，地勤人員務必向旅客明確地告知改訂後抵達目的地時間，好讓旅客能夠重新安排行程。

2-6 奧客硬要排在商務艙優先登機

情境介紹

尚未到登機時間，地勤人員正在拉起排隊用列隊線繩索，有位先生欲進入商務艙及會員專用登機道，地勤人員請他離開。

情境對話 Track 31

M ▸ Michelle，C ▸ Mr. Chen

M: Sir, may I remind you this pathway is for elder passengers or those with infants, and business class passengers. Can I have a look at your boarding pass?

C: Why do you want my boarding pass?

M: Just to make sure that you are at the right place.

C: You will see it later when boarding!

(10 minutes later)

Announce: Passengers on HJ768 to Tokyo are now boarding at gate 22.

(At priority pathway)

M: Sir, now may I have a look at your boarding pass?

C: Here.

M: Sorry, sir. Your seat is economy class. Please queue from the side.

C: Hey! I have been here for over 10 minutes!

M: Yes, but this pathway is for those who have needs and business class passengers. Please go this way.

C: You are really stubborn! I am here already! Can't I just enter by this pathway?! That queue is so long already! I have been waiting here for over 10 minutes! Don't be silly.

M: I'm sorry, sir. But I have informed you before. I'm sorry that you need to queue from the end of the long queue. Actually, if you have waited on the right queue in the beginning, you could be in the cabin already.

C: Ridiculous! What is your name!? I'm going to make a customer complaint on you!

M: I'm sorry about your dissatisfaction. Here is my name. Now please go that way, and thank you for your cooperation.

譯文

M: 先生，提醒您，這個走道是給年紀稍長或是有嬰兒同行，及商務艙的乘客專用的。可以讓我看一下您的登機證嗎？

C: 幹嘛要我的登機證？

M: 只是要確認您站對地方了。

C: 你等一下登機的時候就看得到了！

（10 分鐘後）

廣播：搭乘 HJ768 往東京的旅客，請於 22 號門登機。

（在優先登機走道）

M: 先生，現在我可以看一下您的登機證了嗎？

C: 拿去。

M: 抱歉，先生。您的座位是在經濟艙。請由另外一頭排隊。

C: 喂！我已經在這等了超過 10 分鐘了耶！

M: 是，但這個走道是給有特別需要及商務艙乘客的。請您這邊走。

C: 你真的很盧捏！我已經在這了！不能就讓我從這裡進去嗎？那邊已經排那麼長了！我已經在這等超過 10 分鐘了捏！不要傻了。

M: 我很抱歉，先生。但我剛剛已經跟您說了。我很遺憾您要從那條隊伍的盡頭開始排。事實上，若您一開始就排在對的隊伍，您現在已經在機艙裡了。

C: 太蠢了吧！你叫什麼名字！？我要對你提出客訴！

M: 對於您的不滿，我感到很遺憾。這是我的名字。請您這邊走，並謝謝您的合作。

英文母語者這麼說

Just to make sure that you are at the right place.（只是要確認您站對地方了。）

> 若腦袋裡面先想中文的話，很容易冒出「卡住」，或是出現 *you stand at the right place* 這樣的句子，要特別小心。

字彙解析

- **pathway** *n.* 徑、小路、走道

  I know a secret pathway from here to my house.（我知道一條祕密小徑從這裡通到我家。）

- **remind** *v.* 提醒

  He reminds me of the deadline of homework.（他提醒我作業的期限。）

- **stubborn** *adj.* 固執的

  She gets older and more stubborn.（她變老又變固執了。）

- **silly** *adj.* 愚蠢的

  I was so silly that I forgot to bring my mobile phone.（我真是愚蠢才會忘記帶我的手機。）

- **inform** *v.* 告知、通知

  The manager informed her that she was hired.（那經理通知她，她被錄取了。）

- **ridiculous** *adj.* 荒謬的

  He had a ridiculous life when he was young.（他年輕時過了一段荒謬的生活。）

- **complaint** *n.* 投訴、抱怨

  He got a complaint of his dog from his neighbor.（他鄰居跟他抱怨他的狗。）

補充片語

❶ have a look at 看一看

例 She had a look at my bag and led me go inside the building.（她看了看我的包包，就引導我進到建築物裡。）

❷ make sure 確認

例 She would like to make sure her reservation is okay.（她想確認一下她的預約是沒問題的。）

In Other Words

❶ Can I have a look at your boarding pass? = May I glance at your boarding pass?（我可以看一下您的登機證嗎？）

解 have a look at 是「稍微看一下」、「瞄一眼」，不是看得很仔細的動作，同樣的 glance at 也是這個意思，所以我們可以用 glance at 替代 have a look at。而前面有提過，開頭使用 may I 是較為客氣的說法，然而在文中因地勤人員已經察覺有點不對，

因此僅使用 can I 為開頭，表現出有一點不那麼客氣的口氣了。

地勤工作解說

有些乘客很投機。有時候他們是好奇當一個有優先權的乘客是什麼樣的，或是只是想不付錢又可以有一些特權。這會讓那些付錢的人感到不開心。然而，要同時做到公平又免除爭執不是簡單的事。如文中的情況，地勤人員一開始可能會客氣的請乘客到對的走道，但當這位乘客表現得很防禦時，這位地勤就意識到了，然後轉為堅定地告知他，就是要制止他的行為。

前輩經驗巧巧說

有些乘客在登機門時，看到地勤人員開始拉紅線，就會要站到線內，但其實開始排線只是做準備，還沒有要登機。尤其經濟艙與商務艙會有不同的走道，有些人不清楚或是想混進去，就會走到商務艙的入口。此時，地勤人員會稍微瞄一下客人手中的登機證，因為登機證上設計有不同顏色的區塊，若座位號碼標在商務艙的色塊，即為商務艙乘客，很容易辨認。而文中的先生很取巧的把登機證收起來了，所以地勤才會跟他要登機證。而到了登機時間，這位先生才被發現應該是經濟艙客人，地勤還是請他到另一頭排隊，而為了讓在他後面的商務艙乘客順利入艙，其他地勤人員就會上來補位，為這些客人過登機證，才不會因為一位客人堵住登機口。這些細節都需要整個團隊的默契，才不會延誤班機起飛。

Part 3 入境

3-1 OK Board 入境補辦手續

情境介紹

速達航空公司香港站的地勤 Patty，打電話給台中站的地勤 Michael 詢問香港籍旅客郭先生的入境台灣的簽證問題。

情境對話 Track 32

P ▸ Patty，M ▸ Michael

P: This is Patty, calling from Speedy Air at Hong Kong. We would like to ask an ok board case about Taiwan entry permit.

M: Ok, can I ask what the nationality of this passenger is?

P: This passenger's nationality is China and he holds a Hong Kong passport.

M: Has this passenger applied for the Taiwan entry permit?

P: Yes, he has already applied the permit through the website of Taiwan immigration.

M: Could you fax the passport, Hong Kong ID card and Taiwan entry permit of this passenger to our office?

P: Sure, we're going to fax all documents about this passenger to your office. Please wait for a moment.

M: Thank you. I've received your fax. Is this passenger named Kwok Siu Fong?

P: Correct. As you can see, the place of birth on his passport is Guangdong, however, the place of birth on the entry permit that is Hong Kong.

M: Yes, I also found the difference. We need to inquire whether Mr. Kwok is able to enter Taiwan with this permit; therefore, we're going to ask Taiwan immigration. I'll get back to you after we receive the reply from them.

(After 5 minutes)

M: Hello, this is calling from Taichung airport. Mr. Kwok is allowed to entry Taiwan with the holding of this permit according to the reply of immigration; however, please advise that Mr. Kwok go to Taiwan immigration office for correcting the place of birth on his entry permit when arriving at Taichung.

P: Is there any surcharge to be paid?

M: Yes, please tell Mr. Kwok to prepare TWD 300.

P: I see. I'll inform him.

譯文

P: 我是速達航空香港站的 Patty，想詢問一個關於入境台灣許可證的問題。

M: 好的，請問旅客的國籍是哪裡？

P: 這位旅客是中國籍但持有香港特別行政區護照。

M: 這位旅客已經申請了入台許可證嗎？

P: 有，他已透過台灣移民署網站申請了入台證。

M: 你可以傳真旅客的護照和香港身分證到我們的辦公室嗎？

P: 當然可以，我們馬上傳真有關這位旅客的資料到你們的辦公室。請等一下。

M: 謝謝，我已收到你的傳真。旅客的名字是郭曉風嗎？

P: 是的，沒錯。就如同你所看到，他的護照上面出生地是廣東，但入台證上面是香港。

M: 是的，我也發現不同之處。我們需要詢問關於郭先生是否能用這張入台許可證入境台灣，等我收到他們的回覆後會再聯絡你。

（五分鐘後）

M: 哈囉，我是從台中機場打來過來的。根據台灣移民署的回覆，郭先生可以持這張入台證入境台灣，但是抵達目的時，請郭先生務必先到台灣移民署辦公室，修正入台證上的出生地。

P: 需要額外付費嗎？

M: 需要喔，請告知郭先生準備台幣三百元。

P: 好的，我明白。我會告知他。

英文母語者這麼說

（他已透過台灣移民署網站申請了入台證。）

中式英文：He already has applied the permit in the website of Taiwan immigration.

正確說法：He has already applied the permit through the website of Taiwan immigration.

「already 已經」經常和完成式一起使用，而放入現在完成式的句子應放在 have 後面一般動詞前面，不能將 already 放在 have 的前面。「website 網站」的介系詞不能用 in，應該為 on website，但此句強調是透過網站，因此可用 through 透過。

字彙解析

- **nationality** *v.* 國籍

  Her husband's nationality is British.（她的先生國籍是英國。）

- **fax** *v.* 傳真

  Mary forgot to fax her application form to the college.（Mary 忘記傳真她的申請表到那間學院。）

- **receive** *v.* 收到；接到

  Louis has received this parcel on this Tuesday.（Louis 已經在這星期二收到包裹了。）

- **moment** *n.* 瞬間；片刻

He will be ready in just a moment.（她一會兒就準備好了。）

- **birth** *n.* 出生

You will be asked for the place of birth when applying visa.（當你申請簽證時會要求填出生地。）

- **difference** *n.* 不同；區別；差別

It is difficult to recognize the difference about the twin sisters.（很難分辨這對雙胞胎姊妹的不同之處。）

- **inquiry** *v.* 詢問

If you have any question about law, you would make an inquiry to this lawyer.（如果你有任何有關法律上的問題，你可以詢問這位律師。）

- **response** *n.* 回覆，反應

Gary got good response of this proposal from his boss.（Gary 從他的老闆那得到此企劃案的好反應。）

補充片語

❶ make an inquiry about / into 詢問；打聽

例 Our boss asked me to make an inquiry into other supplier for reducing the cost.（我們的老闆要求我詢問其他供應商減低成本。）

❷ according to 根據；按照

例 Employers will give bonus to the staff according to their performance.（雇主將根據員工的工作表現來給予紅利。）

In Other Words

❶ We need to make an inquiry about Mr. Kwok is suitable for entry Taiwan with this permit; therefore, we are going to ask Taiwan immigration. =We need to get approval from Taiwan immigration about Mr. Kwok is suitable to entry Taiwan with this permit.

（我們需要詢問關於郭先生是否能用這張入台許可證入境台灣，因此我們需要問台灣移民署。）

解 原文中的句意就是要表達我們必須要得到台灣移民署的許可，才能讓此位旅客入境台灣，因此我們可用『get approval from Taiwan immigration 從台灣移民署得到批准』就可省略後面 we are going to ask Taiwan immigration 的句子。

❷ Mr. Kwok is allowed to entry Taiwan with holding this permit according to Taiwan immigration. =Mr. Kwok is allowed to entry Taiwan with this permit in accordance with Taiwan immigration.

（根據台灣移民署規定郭先生可以持這張入台證入境台灣。）

解 according to 此片語可用「in accordance with 根據；按照；依照」來替換，此片語也較為正式。

地勤工作解說

各個國家所規定的簽證和入境許可證形式都不同，各地區的航站會因為旅客所持的簽證內容而有疑慮時，會詢問入境國家的移民署來判斷旅客是否能入境。航空的工作術語稱為『OK BOARD』。入境航站的地勤需要取得客人所持證件的資料再去詢問當地移民署，經移民署官員批准後，再通知外站地勤人員旅客是否能上飛機。

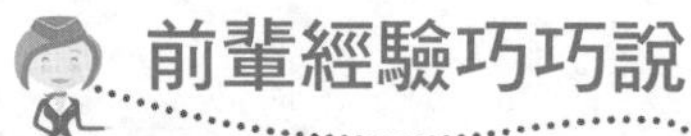

前輩經驗巧巧說

此篇對話中，持有香港護照的旅客可至台灣移民署網站申請入台許可證，但有時因為旅客自行輸入的個人資料與護照上的有出入，例如出生地不同於護照上註明的，擔心旅客可能會因此而無法入境當地，通常地勤人員會將客人所有的旅遊證件傳至目的地航站辦公室再轉由去詢問當地移民署的許可。然而，由於當地移民署有時案件眾多，可能無法在該旅客原定的航班起飛前回覆給航空公司，這時就得告知旅客改搭下一個航班了。地勤人員可別因為航班時間緊迫，擅自將持有問題證件的旅客受理劃位，會因而導致旅客被遣返，造成更大的過失。

3-2 協助轉機

情境介紹

一位老太太要從高雄出發至香港轉機，目的地是上海。因為第一次獨自旅行，因此子女們在辦理登機時請地勤人員特別提供協助。

情境對話 Track 33

(At check in counter)

J ▸ Jason，C ▸ Mrs. Chung，M ▸ Mom，A ▸ Allie

C: My mother is going to Shanghai by herself. Can you assist her to transit via Hong Kong?

J: No problem. Would you like to have a wheelchair service here and Hong Kong, Mrs. Chung?

M: No, it's fine. I can walk.

J: But madam, the distance between gate and gate in Hong Kong is quite far, and it's free of charge. I personally suggest you to have it. Moreover, if you don't want it in Hong Kong, it's fine to cancel it there.

C: He's right, mom. Please give her a wheelchair. Thank you.

J: No problem. Here are your baggage receipt and boarding passes for two sectors. And please have this sticker on your sleeve. Having this sticker on your sleeve will help our Hong Kong staff to find you.

M: Okay, thank you. But how do they know I am going to make a transit via Hong Kong? Should I make a phone call to Hong Kong?

J: Don't worry, madam. Based on the note I mark in our system, our colleagues will soon understand and telegram Hong Kong about your itinerary.

(The flight arrives at Gate 68, Hong Kong airport, ground staff, Allie is waiting for Mrs. Chung)

A: Good morning, madam. Are you Mrs. Chung who is going to Shanghai?

M: Yes, it's me.

A: I'm Allie. I'll lead you to the next boarding gate. If you need anything during this period, please don't hesitate to ask me.

譯文

（在辦理登機櫃台）

C: 我媽媽要自己去上海。可以請你們協助她在香港轉機嗎？

J: 沒問題。您想要在這裏及香港的輪椅服務嗎，鍾太太？

M: 不，不用。我可以走。

J: 但夫人，香港機場登機門與登機門之間的距離相當遠，而且這服務不收費。我個人建議您使用，況且若您在香港不想要了，可以在現場取消沒問題。

C: 她說得對，媽。請給她個輪椅吧，謝謝。

J: 沒問題。這是您的行李收據和兩段航程的登機證。請把貼紙貼在您的袖子上。這是幫助我們香港工作人員可以找到您。他們會陪同您去轉機。

M: 好的，謝謝。但他們怎麼知道我要去香港轉機？我要打個電話給香港嗎？

J: 別擔心，夫人。我會在系統裡做個筆記好讓我的同事們知道，然後他們會打電報去香港告知您的行程。

（飛機抵達香港機場 68 號門，地勤人員 Allie 在等候鍾太太。）

A: 早安，夫人。請問您是要前往上海的鍾太太嗎？

M: 是，我是。

A: 我叫 Allie。我將引導您到下一個登機門。如果您在這段時間需要什麼，可以直接跟我說。

英文母語者這麼說

Please have this sticker on your sleeve.（請把貼紙貼在你的袖子上。）

> have to 常用在一些被動的句子裡。英文常常會使用被動語句來表示一些動作，常常用到的「使~」的動詞就是 have，另一個常用的則是 made。本句請不要講成 Please stick the sticker on your sleeve。

Should I make a phone call to Hong Kong?（我要打個電話給香港嗎？）

> 中文裡我們常說「你再 call 我」表示「你再打給我」的意思，因此大家也很熟悉 call 就是「打電話」的意思。但是若在英文句子裡遇到「打個電話」，請小心不是 call a phone call，是 make a phone call。

字彙解析

- **assist** *v.* 協助

  I was asked to assist my manager during high season.（旺季的時候我被要求去協助我們經理。）

- **distance** *n.* 距離

  It is a long distance from my home to New York.（從我家到紐約有一段很長的距離。）

- **quite** *adv.* 相當

  It is quite cold today.（今天相當冷。）

- **sector** *n.* 部分；本文指航程

  This sector belongs to him, but he emigrated to Canada years ago.（這部分是屬於他的，但他很多年前就移居加拿大了。）

- **sleeve** *n.* 袖子

  There is a hole on your sleeve.（你袖子上有一個洞。）

- **telegram** *v.* 打電報

  My grandpa's work was to telegram for public.（我爺爺的工作是幫大家打電報。）

- **hesitate** *v.* 猶豫

  She did not hesitate to sit by him.（她毫不猶豫就坐在他旁邊。）

補充片語

❶ lead sb. to 帶領…到

例 To my surprise, the first stop that tour guide led us to is a duty-free shop.（那個導遊帶我們去的第一站竟然是免稅店。）

In Other Words

❶ Should I make a phone call to Hong Kong? = Should I call Hong Kong?（我要打個電話給香港嗎？）

解 如果要避免上述提到的說成 call a phone call，你可以選擇簡單的說 Should I call Hong Kong 就好了。

❷ If you need anything during this period, please don't hestitate to ask me. = If you need anything during this period, please feel free to ask me.（如果您在這段時間需要什麼，可以直接跟我說。）

解 本句後段若直譯中文是「請不要猶豫，來問我」，但中文沒有人這麼說，實際上就是「請直接跟我說」的意思。英文裡這句話也可以用 feel free「感到自由的」代替 don't hesitate。

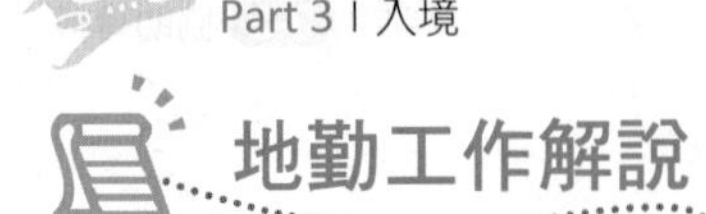

地勤工作解說

若乘客是獨自飛行，或這是他的／她的第一次出國，或是可將這兩個狀況合在一起，我們在機場可以提供於旅程中協助的服務。在出發地的地勤人員會在系統裡做個筆記，好讓所有的工作人員可以用電腦查詢。然後負責發電報的人員會將相關資訊送到轉機的機場，好讓轉機點的工作人員能作安排。

前輩經驗巧巧說

通常我們在機場遇到需要協助的乘客，都是年紀較長的，或是年紀較小但不符合「獨自飛行的孩童」的定義的獨行乘客。在辦理登機時，若乘客提出需要協助轉機，在櫃台備有特別的貼紙，在給登機證及行李收據時一併交給乘客，請他們貼在胸前或是手臂上，下飛機時，轉機點的地勤人員就可以一眼認出需要協助轉機的乘客是哪一位。而地勤人員只要在登機時於該乘客的訂位紀錄中作個筆記，當天發電報的同事就會主動將此資訊傳給轉機點的同事，讓他們安排協助轉機的工作。若兩段航程是搭乘同一家航空，通常沒有特殊狀況，都會在出發地就將兩段航程的登機證印出來，以便乘客到轉機點不用再次辦理登機。這樣的話轉機點的工作人員只要陪同乘客至下一個登機門。但若是搭乘不同航空，需要再次辦理登機，那麼工作人員就會引導乘客到轉機櫃台辦理。

3-3 行李箱損壞求償

情境介紹

旅客 Ivy 抵達目的後於行李轉盤處拿到行李時，發現行李上的把手脫落，因此至航空公司入境櫃檯尋求地勤人員 Gary 協助。

情境對話 Track 34

I ▸ Ivy，G ▸ Gary

I: I just took my check-in luggage from the carousel, but I found the handle of my bag is broken. This is the first time I've used this baggage. How can you compensate it to me?

G: Sorry to cause this problem. Don't worry, madam, we'll take this responsibility. Let me see this bag.

I: Here it is.

G: Ok, the top handle of this luggage is unusable. Let me take a photo to record the extent of this damaged bag. Later, we need your assistance to fill personal information in this form. May I have your passport and bag receipt?

I: Here you go.

G: Thank you, madam. We'll inform the staff in the baggage repair store to go to your home for collecting this damaged bag; hence, please leave your home address and phone number on the form. The staff will contact you before proceeding to your home.

I: Ok, I see. How long does it take?

G: About two weeks. Do you need to use this luggage urgently?

I: Yes, I need it by next Friday because I'll go abroad next Sunday.

G: Ok, your bag will be on our priority list and you'll receive it by next Friday. Here is the form to you and please keep it until your bag is returned. Please do not hesitate to contact us if you have any questions. We do apologize to you sincerely.

譯文

I: 我剛剛從行李運輸帶拿到我的托運行李，但我發現我行李上的把手壞掉了。這是我第一次使用這個行李。請問你們如何賠償我？

G: 很抱歉造成這個問題。不用擔心，我們將會負起責任。讓我來看看您的行李箱。

I: 在這裡。

G: 好的，這行李箱上面的把手確實已無法使用。讓我來拍照記錄一下這件行李箱的損壞範圍。待會也得需要您的協助幫我們填張表格。我可以向您先借護照和行李收據嗎？

I: 給你。

G: 謝謝您，女士。我們將通知維修行李店的員工前往您的住所拿取這件行李，因此請在表格上留下您的地址和聯絡電話。工作人員在前往您家之前會與您聯繫。

I: 好的，我明白了。我的行李需要花多少時間修理好？

G: 它需要耗時兩週。您有急著要這行李嗎？

I: 是，我必須在下週五之前收到它因為我下週日要出國。

G: 好的，您的行李將會被優先處理且您將會下週五收到。這個表格給您請您保留好直到您的行李回來為止。如您有任何問題請別猶豫立即跟我們聯絡。由衷地向您再次道歉。

英文母語者這麼說

（這是我第一次使用這個行李。）

中式英文：At the first time, I use this baggage.

正確說法：This is the first time I've used this baggage.

「第一次」不要用 at the first time 英文無此說法，第一次應該直接說 the first time。此外，這個行李箱已經開始使用了，所以動詞應用現在完成式來表達，而非現在式。

（您有急著要用這行李嗎？）

中式英文：Do you hurry to use this baggage?

正確說法：Do you need to use this baggage urgently?

「急著」不能用 hurry，因為 hurry 是動詞「加快、催促、匆忙」的意思，如果用 hurry to use 會變成「快把它用掉」與「急著要用」意思完全不同。正確說法用 urgently 為副詞「急切地」且放在句尾。

- **handle** *n.* 把手

  Do not touch the handle of kettle when boiling water.（當水滾開時不要碰那茶壺的把手。）

- **compensate** *v.* 賠償

  John has to compensate this victim by this car incident.（John必須對這次車禍中的受害者賠償。）

- **responsibility** *n.* 責任

  The manager needs to take this responsibility for this negligence.（經理需要對這次的過失負起責任。）

- **record** *v.* 記錄；錄製

  We invite this photographer to record our wedding.（我們邀請一位專業攝影師來錄製我們的婚禮。）

- **extent** *n.* 範圍；程度

  The doctor examines the extent of his injuries.（這位醫生檢查他的受傷程度。）

- **damaged** *adj.* 受損的

  Both scooters are damaged by this car accident.（因為這場車禍這兩台機車都是受損的。）

- **repair** *v.* 修理

  My father repairs the window after typhoon.（我的爸爸在颱風過後修理窗戶。）

- **urgently** *adv.* 急切地；迫切地

  He needs the help urgently.（他急切地需要幫忙。）

- **hesitate** *v.* 猶豫

  Stacy doesn't hesitate to agree this proposal.（Stacy 毫無猶豫答應求婚。）

補充片語

❶ fill...in 填入

例 Please fill your contact details in this phone book.（請填寫您的聯絡資料到這本電話簿。）

❷ go abroad 出國

例 Joanna always goes abroad with her mom.（Joanna 總是和她的媽媽一起出國。）

Memo

In Other Words

❶ Sorry to cause this problem. = We apologize for this problem caused.（很抱歉造成這個問題。）

解 apologize 也是「道歉」的意思，比起 sorry 更為正式用語。換句話中可用被動式來強調出問題被製造出來。

❷ We'll inform the staff in the baggage repair store to go to your home for collecting this damaged bag, hence please leave your home address and phone number on the form. = Please leave your home address and phone number on the form because we'll inform our staff in the baggage repair store to go to your home for collecting this bag.

（我們將通知維修行李店的員工前往您的住所拿取這件行李，因此請在表格上留下您的地址和聯絡電話。）

解 換句話説中，先將請求旅客的事項説出來，請求旅客留下聯絡方式，而後再慢慢向客人可能解釋為何要這麼做。可直接點名此句子的目的。

地勤工作解說

托運行李在運送過程中難免會因為行李運輸帶機器的碰撞，導致行李受損。航空公司都會在入境行李轉盤旁設置服務櫃檯以便讓旅客拿完行李後立即發現行李受損而尋求協助，地勤人員會依照行李受損情形來判斷行李是否能夠修復，如輪子脫落、把手損壞等狀況還在可修復範圍內，因此會請旅客留下聯絡資料，先讓旅客回家後整理出行李箱內的物品，再請專業修復行李人員前往旅客家中收取行李，一旦修理好的行李回來後，再將行李箱送回給旅客。

前輩經驗巧巧說

如果旅客的行李箱嚴重損壞而導致連行李維修公司都無法修理的話，航空公司人員便會與旅客談有限的賠償,例如：就旅客行李箱使用的折舊率、行李箱價值、樣式、功能性上有限的去賠償旅客，通常旅客使用的一般行李箱嚴重損壞的話，航空公司也會直接的賠償一個新的行李箱或些許的現金賠償給客人去自行維修或購買新的行李箱。所以旅客若有一個 RIMOWA 之類的精品行李箱嚴重損壞的話，航空公司大多也僅會依照公司及國際公約的規範下進行有限的金額賠償，故一個兩、三萬塊的行李箱嚴重損壞不能再用時航空公司也無法賠償客人一個等值的新行李箱。依照地勤本人看過無數行李箱損壞的經驗，沒有什麼行李箱是不會壞的也未必貴就是比較好！只有堅固和耐用的分別而已，行李箱也盡量避免空箱托運！至少將行李箱裝至七分滿，這樣一來行李箱在裝載堆疊的過程中被其他行李箱壓上去裡面的內容物也會提供足夠的支撐而比較不會被其他過重的行李箱所壓壞。

3-4 旅客遺失行李

情境介紹

一位女性旅客 Emma Conway 從倫敦搭機抵台，在行李轉盤等候了十幾分鐘仍未領到其中一件託運行李，便主動到行李服務櫃台向地勤職員洽詢。

情境對話 Track 35

D ▸ Daniel，E ▸ Emma

E: I've been waiting for my check-in baggage for 15 minutes, but I am not able to find it. Can you help me with it?

D: May I have your passport and your baggage claim tag? A check-in baggage receipt you get from the check in agent at the counter.

E: Here you are.

D: May I confirm with you that your flight is S250 departed from London Heathrow Airport on 8 July, and there are two check-in baggage?

E: Yes. I do receive one of them, but I cannot find the second one on the carousel.

D: Which one did you receive? May I take a look at your baggage tag?

E: (Show her bag to the ground staff) How did it happen? It never happens to me!

D: We apologize for it. There are many reasons for missing baggage. Tight connection, tag missing, check in error. I'll try my best to find it, so I need some information from you. Please fill in this form here.

E: (Filling in the form) Can I write down the hotel address instead of my home address? I don't live in Taiwan.

D: Sure. To locate your baggage easier, please describe your baggage for record such as color, size or material.

E: It's a Rimowa brown suitcase made of Polycarbonate.

D: I see. I'll put all the details in the record and we can find it easier.

E: How long does it take to find my baggage?

D: I'm afraid we aren't sure about it. Once we find it, we'll contact you and deliver it to your hotel as soon as possible. Here is a copy of your baggage missing profile. Please keep it until we locate your bag.

譯文

E: 不好意思，我已經等我的托運行李十五分鐘了但是我沒看到它。你可以幫我嗎？

D: 好的，小姐。我可以跟您借護照和行李領取單嗎？就是您會從櫃台劃位人員那拿到一張行李收據。

E: 在這裏。

D: 我可以再次向您確認你的航班是 7 月 8 號 S250 從倫敦希斯洛機場？有兩件行李託運是嗎？

E: 是的，沒錯。我只拿到了一件行李，但是我沒在轉盤上看到第二件。

D: 請問您拿到的是哪一件？我能看一下您的行李條嗎？

E: （給地勤人員看她領到的行李）怎麼會這樣？我從來沒發生過這樣的情況。

D: 非常抱歉，Conway 女士。有很多原因造成行李遺失。轉機時間太短、行李條脫落、掛錯行李。我們將盡全力找行李。因此，我需要您的資訊。請幫我填妥這表格。

E: 好的。（填表格中）我可以寫下我住的飯店地址來替代我家地址嗎？我不是住在台灣。

D: 當然可以。為了更快找到您的行李，也麻煩您形容您的行李箱以便我們做記錄。舉例來說，顏色、尺寸或材質。

E: 它是咖啡色的 Rimowa 行李箱，由塑膠材質做成的。

D: 我明白了，我將這些細節記錄起來，方便我們找它。

E: 多久會找到我的行李？

D: 我們恐怕無法跟您確認多久，但我們將會盡全力找尋。一旦我們找到了，會跟您連絡並盡快將行李送到您的飯店。十分抱歉造成您的不便。這是您行李遺失資料的副本。請留著直到我們找到行李為止。

英文母語者這麼說

（有很多原因造成行李遺失。）

中式英文：Many reasons are missing baggage.

正確說法：There are many reasons for missing baggage.

中式英文的句意會變成『很多理由是遺失行李。』完全表達錯誤。there is 來表達有後面再加上詞 for，句意和文法才是正確完整。

字彙解析

- **claim** *v.* 領取

  His son asks to claims the land.（他的兒子要求領取這塊土地。）

- **tight** *adj.* 緊的

  We would like to have a meeting with the manager; however, he has a very tight schedule.（我們想跟經理開會但是他的行程安排很緊。）

- **error** *n.* 錯誤

  There are some typing errors in this book.（這本書有一些打字錯誤。）

- **polycarbonate** *n.* 聚碳酸酯（塑膠材質的一種）

  I think the best material of the suitcase is made by polycarbonate.（我認為最好的行李箱材質是聚碳酸酯。）

補充片語

❶ instead of 代替；取代

例 John will take this case instead of you.（John 將取代你接這個案子。）

In Other Words

❶ May I confirm with you that your flight is 250 departed from London Heathrow Airport on 8 July? = Is your flight S250 from London Heathrow Airport on 8 July?

解 省略了 May I confirm with you 直接詢問客人這個航班好是否正確更簡單明瞭。

地勤工作解說

造成旅客行李遺失的原因有很多種，常見的有幾種狀況：轉機銜接的航班太趕、行李牌脫落 、行李未直掛到終點站、航班延誤異常另行更改旅客的航班路線、行李運送人員或旅客劃位人員疏失，航空公司會請旅客留下地址和電話號碼，以便當行李找到時直接運送到旅客住所。

前輩經驗巧巧說

如果旅客的行李是因為時間緊迫而錯過續程航班時，航空公司人員皆會在該行李條上貼上 RUSH TAG（立即後送的標籤），之後以當前時間最近的航班盡速將行李送往該旅客的目的地。若旅客的行李因掉牌等原因而使得該件行李不知送往何處時，當站處理行李的航空公司人員會依照此行李的外觀、特徵、顏色、重量、品牌、內容物等詳盡的記載後，將此行李建立一個 OHD CASE（ON HAND）失物招領的檔案，供全世界各個航空公司依旅客所申報行李遺失的特徵來進行比對，之後航空公司會以比對結果的吻合率，來判斷是否跟該建立無身份行李的航站請求，將此行李送到客人的抵達站與客人來進行更詳盡的比對。

Part 4 特殊狀況處理

4-1 乘客遺留物品在機上

情境介紹

一位女性旅客 Emily 從上海搭機抵台，下機後，走了一段路才發現遺失了一個皮夾在機上，便急忙返回欲上機尋找，遇見剛剛接機的地勤職員 Allen。

情境對話 Track 36

E ▸ Emily，A ▸ Allen

E: Excuse me. I think I left a wallet in the cabin. Can I return to my seat now?

A: Miss, may I see your boarding pass, please?

E: Oh, I think I might have put it in the front seat pocket! Will that be a problem?

A: It's okay, but do you still remember your seat number?

E: I don't remember exactly, but it might be around 30A or 31 A.

A: A window seat?

E: Yes, that is correct.

A: How does your wallet look like?

E: It is dark brown, and with LV logo on it.

A: Okay, please wait here at the arrival gate. I'll contact my colleague and see if we can find it.

(In the meantime, Allen uses the walkie-talkie to contact her Ramp Coordinator, David)

A: David, there is a passenger who left her wallet in the cabin. Seat number 30A or 31A.

(2 minutes later)

A: Miss, is this the wallet you left behind?

E: Yes, yes! It's mine.

A: Due to the safety procedure, would you please show me your passport and also provide an identity card from your wallet, to confirm it is yours?

E: Sure, this is my passport, and this is my ID card.

A: (carefully check the name on both documents) Thank you, Miss. Now you can have your wallet back. Please also kindly check your wallet and see if there is anything else missing.

E: Okay, I think everything is here. I really appreciate with your help!

譯文

E: 不好意思，我的皮夾似乎掉在機上，我可以回到座位上找找看嗎？

A: 好的，小姐，那可以借我看一下您的登機證嗎？

E: 我好像把登機證遺留在前座的袋子了！會不會怎樣？

A: 沒關係，那您記得您的座位號碼嗎？

E: 我不太記得了，不過可能是 30A 或 31A 附近 。

A: 是個靠窗的位子嗎？

E: 是的，沒錯。

A: 請問小姐您的皮夾特徵是？

E: 它是深咖啡色的，上面有個 LV 的標誌。

A: 好的，那請您在入境閘口稍候一下，我請同事幫您找看看！

（此時，Angel 使用對講機呼叫機邊督導）

A: 呼叫 David，有一名旅客遺失皮夾在機上，座位在 30A 或是 31A。

（兩分鐘後）

A: 小姐，請問這個是您遺失的皮夾嗎？

E: 對對，這是我的。

A: 好，但因為安全程序上的關係，可以請您借我您的護照及皮夾中的證件，以驗證是您的嗎？

E: 當然沒問題，這是我的護照及身分證。

A: （仔細檢查證件）謝謝您，小姐，您可以拿回您的皮夾了。麻煩您也確認一下皮夾內的所有物是否都在。

E: 好的，我想應該沒有掉東西。非常感謝你的幫忙！

英文母語者這麼說

I don't remember exactly.

（我記不太清楚了。）

exactly 的中文是確切地，精確地。此作為修飾動詞的副詞，強調「不是記得地很精確」、「記得的不是那麼清楚了」，比 I don't remember 所代表的「我不記得了」還婉轉、含糊。此文中，旅客 Emily 說 I don't remember exactly，表示她並非完全忘記，只是不確定、依稀記得座位大概是 30A 或 31A。

There is a passenger who left her wallet in the cabin.

（有一名旅客遺失了皮夾在機上。）

此句常被國人誤用為 There have a passenger...表示中文的「有」一名旅客。但英文母語者不會使用這樣的句子，若要表示「有」一名旅客在機上、「有」一隻貓咪在樹上、「有」一枝筆在桌上，都會用 There is/are 為句首開頭。

例 1：您的機票有更改限制。

錯誤→Your flight ticket has restrictions.

正確→There are some restrictions on your flight ticket.

例 2：本航班有一名年紀大的輪椅旅客。

錯誤→This flight has an elderly wheelchair passenger.

正確→There is an elderly wheelchair passenger on this flight.

字彙解析

- **seat pocket** 椅背置物袋；座椅口袋

  The airsickness bag is in your seat pocket in front of you.（清潔袋放置於您前方的椅背置物袋。）

- **arrival gate** 入境閘口

  Please wait at the arrival gate where our staff will meet you there.（請在入境閘口稍後，我們的職員會在那等候您。）

- **colleague** *n.* 同事

  Your colleague told me to pay my excess fee here.（你的同事請我在此付超重費。）

- **ramp coordinator** 機邊督導

  One of the duties for the ramp coordinator is to make sure the catering service is completed.（機邊督導的職責之一是確認空廚作業完成。）

- **cabin door** 機艙門

  The cabin door will be closed ten minutes before departure.（機艙門將在起飛前十分鐘關上。）

- **provide** *v.* 提供

  Please provide a copy of your passport to your travel agent.（請提供一份護照影本給您的旅行社代辦人員。）

- **identity** *n.* 身分

  You may apply a landing visa if you hold your identity card and a photo.（您只要持有身分證及照片，就可以申請落地簽證。）

補充片語

❶ confirm something with sb. 與某人…確認某物（事）…

例 Can you confirm the color with the passenger?（妳可以跟旅客確認顏色外觀嗎？）

解 Confirm 的中文詞意為「確認」，若要表達「向某人確認」則須加上介系詞「with」。因為地勤工作時常需與旅客確認不同事項，例如旅客的行程、目的地、座位喜好、簽證、訂位紀錄、登機證上的資訊等等，故職場上常使用此字。

常見的例句是：

May I confirm your itinerary with you?

我可以跟您確認行程嗎？

May I confirm the booking reference with you?

我可以跟您確認您的訂位代號嗎？

Please confirm with your travel agent for your special meal requirement.

請再與您的旅行社確認您預定的特別餐是否無誤。

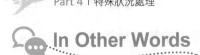

In Other Words

❶（可以借我看一下您的登機證嗎？）

May I see your boarding pass, please?

= May I have your boarding pass, please?

= May I take a look at your boarding pass, please?

解 無論何時何地，當地勤人員要確認旅客身分，最快的方式便是確認旅客的登機證，登機證上的資訊包含登機編號、旅客姓名、座位號碼等等。而重要的是如何有禮貌地向旅客借取登機證，以上列舉的例句皆為禮貌性地請求旅客出示登機證。

❷（可以請您借我驗證您的護照及皮夾中的證件是相符的嗎？）

Would you please show me your passport and also provide an identity card from your wallet, to confirm it is yours? = Would that be possible for you to provide an identity card which matches to your passport? = We would like to confirm your identity by matching the name on your passport with your identity card from your wallet.

解 向旅客核對身分時，務必保持良好態度，避免帶給旅客不好觀感，有禮貌的向旅客提出驗證身分的語氣便極為重要。例如「Would you please…」或是「Would that be possible for your to…」等開頭，皆可保持禮貌地引導出後面主要的洽詢問句。而第三個例句的目的也等同於前兩句，但並非問句，而是先向旅客解說我們基於安全上想確認身分的用意，再用 by…（某種方式）…來引導出我們欲請他提供證件，供我們驗證身分的請求。

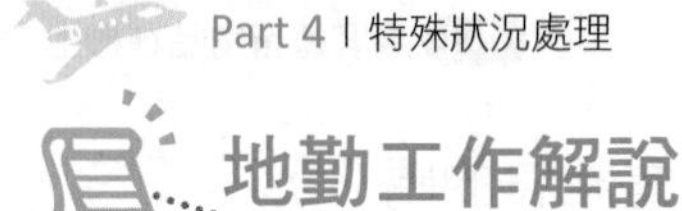

地勤工作解說

當旅客遺忘物品時，地勤的處理方式需小心謹慎。本文中的旅客 Emily 一下機就發現東西遺失，立即折返尋找，此時尋回遺失物品的機率極大，而旅客一旦離開機艙，通常清艙人員會立即登機打掃飛機，而組員也會趁空休息片刻或做下一個航班的準備，通常在未經許可下，不建議讓旅客直接返回機上尋找遺失物，這是為了避免打斷清艙作業，也是安全問題。

上述情境最佳的處理方式，即是向旅客確認遺失物品特徵、遺失地點（座位號碼），再由地勤人員或機上組員替旅客尋找，若找到了則會立即交還與旅客，這時也需立即向旅客確認遺失物品的完整度，尤其是攸關錢財與證件的皮夾，務必在交還旅客當下，請旅客現場確認皮夾內的證件和錢財是否完整無缺。若真有短缺，也好立即回頭追查是否掉在路上或機上。

另一種情況為清艙人員或機上組員發現有旅客遺失的物品，卻等不到旅客當下回頭認領，這時候，不知名的遺失物品就會交由入境地勤人員帶回建檔，需註明航班日期與編號、拾獲位置、物品名稱與特徵品牌、拾獲人員等完整資訊，以供日後旅客電洽尋找此物時，方便同事過濾辨別。旅客離開機場後，若發現有物品遺失，則可返回機場詢問地勤人員，也可以撥打航空公司行李部門或入境部門的電話詢問，每間航空公司都有負責遺失物品管理的單位。

前輩經驗巧巧說

旅客遺失物品中常見的有護照、皮夾、手機、平板電腦、相機、眼鏡、外套、圍巾、書籍、保溫瓶等旅遊用品，而越重要或越有價值的東西，旅客回頭尋找的機率就越高。

最快發現、也是最重要的遺失物品就是護照，因為旅客在提領行李前皆需通過移民署查驗護照，常有旅客在排隊通關時才發現護照遺失，移民署官員會立即撥打電話至航空公司通報，督導或主管會立即透過對講機聯絡入境接機的地勤，尋獲後再送往移民署歸還給旅客，交給旅客前，建議同事需核對護照照片以外、也多詢問旅客一句護照上印有的身分證字號或生日等個資，確保護照交還正確。

4-2 航班因天候因素延誤

情境介紹

一位小姐欲搭機經香港轉機至德國法蘭克福，於櫃檯劃位時得知至香港的班機因天候因素短暫延誤。

情境對話 Track 37

N ▸ Nick，M ▸ Ms. Moore

N: (Checking passport) Ms. Moore. May I confirm with you that your itinerary is KA455 to Hong Kong and connected with LH797 to Frankfurt?

M: That's correct.

N: Thank you Ms. Moore. I'm very sorry to inform you that KA455 is delayed- the incoming flight has been temporarily held up in the Hong Kong International Airport due to unfavorable weather conditions. The expected delay time is about 40 minutes. We'll update the new boarding and departure time with you once the incoming flight has successfully departed from Hong Kong.

M: I see. I've heard that it rains cats and dogs today in Hong Kong. It's okay for me to wait, yet I'm a little concerned with my transfer time in Hong Kong, since I only have about one and a half hours. Is there anything you can do to help me there?

N: Yes, Ms. Moore. We can arrange a "Meet and assist service" in Hong Kong International Airport; when you arrive in Hong Kong, please find our ground staff outside of the cabin, they'll take you to your next boarding gate as soon as possible.

M: That sounds good. Is it possible for this flight to be further delayed?

N: I'm sorry to say this, yet it's indeed possible, since the weather is always unpredictable.

M: I understand. Safety comes first anyway. Would you keep me in the loop?

N: We certainly will, and we are sorry for any inconvenience caused.

M: I'll get my fingers crossed.

譯文

N:（查閱護照）Moore 小姐，能跟您確認一下您的行程是搭程 KA455 至香港，轉 LH797 航班前往法蘭克福嗎？

M: 正確。

N: 謝謝您，Moore 小姐。很抱歉通知您，KA455 往香港的航班有延誤，由香港欲抵台的班機由於天候不佳暫時耽擱在機場，目前預計延誤 40 分鐘；當來機自香港起飛之後，我們會再跟您更新延誤後的登機時間及起飛時間。

M: 我明白了。我已經聽説香港今天雨下得很大。我可以等沒關係，只是我有點擔心我在香港的轉機時間，因為我只有大約一個半小時而已。您能在香港幫我安排一些協助嗎？

N: 沒問題，Moore 小姐。我們將為您安排 MAAS 的協助，請您搭達香港之後聯繫我們機艙外的地勤人員，他們會帶您儘速趕到您下個航班的登機門口。

M: 聽起來不錯。這個班機有沒有可能會延誤更久呢？

N: 雖然很抱歉，但我必須説它的確可能會延誤更久，畢竟天氣狀況是無法預測的。

M: 我了解。總之安全最重要。有新的時間麻煩通知我一聲，可以嗎？

N: 當然沒問題！對您造成不便我們深感抱歉。

M: 我會祈禱航班不會再延誤。

英文母語者這麼說

I'll get my fingers crossed.

我會祈禱（某件事）

由於英文母語者普遍信仰基督教及天主教，對話中如果要祈求某件事或祝人好運，會將食指及中指交叉（也可以說 cross your fingers）代表十字架，除了代表好運之外，也是在祈求心中想的事情可以達成。

字彙解析

- **confirm** *v.* 證實、確定

  Please confirm your full name and birthday on the check list, thank you.（請確認表格上你的全名及生日是否正確，謝謝！）

- **inform** *v.* 通知、告知

  All passengers should be informed that smoking is not allowed in the cabin.（所有旅客皆應被告知機艙內是禁止吸煙的。）

- **unfavorable** *adj.* 不利的、不適宜的

  The air quality today is unfavorable for any kind of outdoor activity.（今天的空氣品質不適合從事任何戶外活動。）

- **concern** *n. v.* 擔心、使不安

  Ms. Moore expresses her concern about the delay of her flight.（Moore 對於她的航班延誤表示擔心。）

  Mark's health condition concerned his parents.（Mark 的健康狀況讓他的父母感到擔心。）

- **indeed** *adv.* （加強語氣）確實、實在

  He is indeed a good friend.（他確實是個很好的朋友。）

- **unpredictable** *adj.* 不可預料的、 出乎意料的

  Our boss is famous for his unpredictable temper.（我們老闆最有名的就是他那不可預料的脾氣。）

補充片語

❶ keep me in the loop 請向我更新進展如何

解 loop 這個字在不同領域有不同的意思，它的本義為「環狀、循環」；而在一般生活口語裡，則常將 loop 用來象徵某個正在進行中，尚未結束的事件或狀況。所以將某人留在某個事件的 loop 裡，延伸的意義就是會持續向某人更新這個事件的動態。

In Other Words

❶ It rains cats and dogs = It rains heavily.

解 It rains cats and dogs 是英文口語常用的諺語，用來指滂沱大雨，意思上和 heavy rain 一樣，只是較為生動，和實際的貓與狗其實並沒有關係。

❷ One and a half hours = one hour and a half

解 口語上較常說 one and a half hours，而書寫時則較常用 one hour and a half。意思上並無差別，只是需要注意 one and a half 後面的 hour 就要加複數 s。另外也需注意並非所有情況都可以此類推，例如：He drank one and a half glasses of water 較為正確則常見，而 He drank a glass and a half of water 相較之下意思雖通，但鮮少使用。

地勤工作解說

在天氣不適合飛行的情況下，一個航班勢必會有所延誤，甚而取消。此時，機場地勤人員便有義務告知旅客相關的訊息，並持續向旅客更新航班動態。由於旅客原訂之行程可能會受到影響，地勤人員也會協助將可能的負面影響降至最低。例如：如果旅客有轉機，並在延誤後仍可能趕上轉機航班，地勤人員便會於轉機機場安排協助轉機的服務；若旅客可能會錯過原訂的航班，地勤人員在當班督導的授權下也可視情況協助旅客重新訂位或更改航班。對於其他旅客，地勤人員也會秉持著服務精神盡可能提供協助及建議。但由於因天候因素造成的延誤通常無法理賠，地勤人員能提供的協助也相對有限。

前輩經驗巧巧說

在機場工作，遇到航班因天候因素而延誤的頻率其實很高，因為各種天氣狀況都可能會影響到飛航的安全。例如豪大雨時因考量跑道狀況及視線不佳等因素，機場常會實施流量管制，進而造成許多航班因此延誤；如果是雷陣雨時甚至會因為閃電而暫停所有地面作業，需等到閃電停歇機長才能趕緊抓準時機起飛。另外在有颱風的情況下更是無法勉強飛行，必須等到機長判斷天氣適合飛行才會有確定的起飛時間。以上原因造成延誤的時間可長可短，但其實分分秒秒的等待地勤人員心裡的焦急都不亞於要旅行的旅客：因為在班機延誤的影響之下，原本有轉機的客人都可能趕不上原本的航班；就算沒有轉機，旅客原本安排好的行程、購買好的交通接駁票卷、預訂好的旅館…等都會跟著受到影響，產生的問題都不好處理。而天候造成的延誤屬於不可抗力因素，一般航空公司皆無法提供相關的賠償，這個時候機場的地勤人員就會是整個飛行計劃裡在最前線接受客人壓力的人員。除了秉持著服務精神盡力協助受影響的旅客之外，也時常要承受許多旅客的負面情緒。記得好幾次在颱風天其他行業都放假在家避難時，我們機場地勤人員還是得想盡辦法冒著風雨在上班時間趕到機場面對客人不間斷的質問與謾罵，次數多了其實難免會造成心裡上的壓力，也只能自己努力調適。

4-3 機械故障：航班取消

情境介紹

登機前 20 分鐘，機長發現駕駛艙某零件鬆脫，便立即通報工程部同事進行維修，同時也透過機邊督導告知登機門地勤人員延誤登機，待工程部同事確認此異常無法立即排除，機長基於飛行安全因素，做出航班取消的決定。

情境對話

Track 38

S ▸ Sarah，M ▸ Mandy，W ▸ Mr. Wang

S: Mandy, please make a flight cancelled announcement in 5 minutes. There will be more staffs coming here to help soon. Remember, your intonation must be calm. Don't start a panic.

M: Okay. (Announcing) Ladies and Gentlemen, may I have your attention please. XX Airways regrets to advise you that the flight XX443 departing for New York has been cancelled due to technical problem. XX Airways apologize for the inconvenience caused. Please kindly remain seated and our staffs at Gate 26 would soon make another flight arrangement for every passenger. Thank You for your understanding.

(Some of the passengers are approaching to Service Desk anxiously)

W: Technical problems? What should I do now? I have an important meeting 3 hours after landing. I must depart today!

M: We apologize for causing your inconvenience, Sir. May I have your passport and the boarding pass?

W: Here you are. Please be hurry.

M: Yes, Mr. Wang. There will be another flight with UU Air departing to New York today. May I transfer you to UU450? The scheduled departure time is 15:30.

W: Let me think about it. So it would be 2 hours later than my original flight?

M: That is correct, and we are sorry for it. If you accept our arrangement, I will contact my colleague and we can re-issue your E-ticket now.

W: I think it is the only way. Okay, fine. I will take it. I also need a flight certificate for your cancellation.

M: Yes, we'll make sure to deliver it to you with your new boarding pass. Thank you, Mr. Wang.

S: Mandy，請妳五分鐘後廣播航班取消的資訊，稍後有更多同事前來支援，記得廣播語調要冷靜些。不要引起恐慌。

M: 各位旅客請注意，XX 航空往紐約的班機 XX443 由於機械故障，將取消起飛，對於造成您的不便，XX 航空深感抱歉，請各位旅客先留在原座，地勤人員將於 26 號登機門協助各位旅客更改後續行程。非常謝謝各位旅客的體諒。

（有幾位旅客焦慮地前來櫃台詢問）

W: 機械故障？那我現在該怎麼辦？我抵達紐約三個小時後就有一場很重要的會議，我一定要今天出發！

M: 好的，先生，很抱歉造成您的困擾，能不能先借我您的護照和登機證呢？

W: 給妳，請快點幫我處理。

M: 好的，王先生，今天出發的另一個航班是 UU 航空的 UU450，起飛時間預計是 15:30，我替您安排那個航班好嗎？

W: 我想看看，所以那班比我原本預定的航班還要晚了兩小時嗎？

M: 是的，真的很抱歉，如果您可以接受這個安排，我會立即請同事替您更改機票。

W: 也只能這樣了，好吧，幫我安排那個航班，我還要一張航班取消證明。

M: 沒問題，王先生，稍後再將航班取消證明與新的登機證一起交給您。

英文母語者這麼說

Here you are.

（給你。）

這是一句在英語中使用率很高、卻很難解釋的一句話，這句話的用途非常廣泛，最常用於「要把某物交給某人」或「向某人出示某物」的場合。是較為口語的用法，中文多翻譯為「給你吧」、「拿去吧」等句。

Please kindly remain seated.

（請您先留在原座。）

一般請人坐下，會說 Please sit down，代表邀請站著的人坐下。但情境劇中，大部分旅客已是坐在登機門休息區，所以使用的句子必須是「維持原座」之意。

而這句話的主要用意是禮貌性的請旅客先留在原座位，提醒旅客稍安勿躁。使用 kindly（副詞）去修飾 remain（動詞），kindly 有好心地、和藹親切地、也有「勞煩您」做某事之意，而 remain 是指「保持」、「留在…」之意，所以此時不建議用 Please sit down，而需用 remain seated。

I will take it.

就這樣替我安排吧／我接受這樣的安排。

這可不是在表示「我要拿它」的意思，take it 原是「忍受」的意思，例如 I cannot take it anymore.代表「我無法再忍受了」、「我受夠了」。而在此情境劇中，王先生表示 I will take it 代表著他其實不得不接受此安排的意思，帶有非自願接受的涵義，中文亦可翻為「好吧，也只能接受了」之意。

字彙解析

- **intonation** *n.* 語調；聲調

It is not appropriate to use a flat intonation when you are doing an announcement.（單調的語調不適合用在正式廣播時。）

- **technical** *adj.* 技術上的

The engineer requires a special technical skill to maintain the aircraft.（負責保養飛機的工程師需具備特殊的技術專長。）

- **arrangement** *n.* 安排；準備

We have already made hotel arrangements for all the delayed passengers.（我們已為所有航班延誤的旅客安排了旅館住宿。）

- **anxiously** *adv.* 焦急地；擔憂地

The girl in front of counter 3 is anxiously calling her parents because she left her passport at home.（三號櫃台前的那位女孩忘了帶護照，正焦急地打電話聯絡父母。）

- **transfer** *v.* 轉移；調動；轉讓

Sir, we would like to transfer you to another earlier flight because of the delay.（先生，由於航班延誤，我們將幫您轉到另一個早一點出發的航班。）

- **certificate** *n.* 證明書；憑證

Excuse me, which counter can I get a flight delay certificate form?（不好意思，我想申請航班延誤證明，請問要到哪個櫃台呢？）

補充片語

❶ start a panic 引起一陣恐慌

例 The explosion has started a panic that everyone is screaming and shouting.（爆炸聲引起了眾人的恐慌，大家都在尖聲叫喊。）

解 panic 的中文為「恐慌；驚慌」，可當作名詞、形容詞或動詞「使…恐慌」使用。

常見的例句是：

Do not panic!（此為動詞）= Don't be panic!（此為形容詞）不要驚慌！

Sarah is comforting the panic passenger who suffered the fire on board.（Sarah 正在安撫那位在機上受到火災驚嚇的旅客。）

The passenger is too panic to take the flight. Do you know the reason?（那位旅客對於搭機這件事感到驚慌，你知道原因嗎？）

In Other Words

❶ Thank You for your understanding.

= We appreciate with your kind understanding.（非常謝謝各位旅客的體諒。）

解 當航班延誤或取消等異常情況發生時，正式廣播的內容資訊必須完整清楚，尤其是結尾不得馬虎，以表達我們的誠心與歉意。此二句的意思相近，都屬於既誠心又禮貌的結尾。

注意的是 thank you 後面介係詞用 for＋動名詞、appreciate 後面介系詞用 with＋動名詞。

❷ We apologize for causing your inconvenience.

=We apologize for your inconvenience caused.

（很抱歉造成您的不便。）

解 無論是面對面向旅客致歉，或於廣播時使用，此兩種說法皆很常見，差異只有文法上的使用方式不同，意思是相同的。apologize 是道歉、認錯之意，常見的用法是 apologize to somebody（某人）for something（某事），所以此句省略了 We apologize (to you) for causing your inconvenience.而最一般口語的反應是直接說 We are sorry for/about it.「對此我們感到很抱歉。」道歉完，記得再接續提供解決辦法給旅客，才不會造成旅客誤解我們完全幫不上忙又沒有誠心要解決，釋出善意和誠意更為重要。

地勤工作解說

航班取消的原因很多種，其中，天氣因素造成的取消比較淺而易見，不論是地勤或旅客也都比較有心理準備。而機械故障或技術性故障等造成的取消往往臨時發生，大部分都在登機前、機長或工程師做最後的準備才發現，所以地勤人員需要面對與處理的責任也相較龐大，考驗的是各位的臨場反應及危機處理。

而處理方式大致如下：最佳情況是現場替旅客安排其他替代航班（自家其他航班，或是外家航空公司），此時需留意旅客的託運行李有幾件，並連絡行李室或航勤人員幫忙更換行李牌，且需確定旅客的行李會送上新的航班上，最後也需將旅客的登機證與行李收據更換成新的。而有些旅客會選擇取消當日航班，改期出發，此時則需替旅客更改其訂位紀錄，並將剛剛已託運的行李領出（需填寫退關單，並連絡行李室與海關人員，共同辦理）

要注意的是，地勤手上提供給旅客的資訊絕對要準確充分，在沒有權力或公司決策未下達前，不可以隨便承諾旅客（例如免費提供旅館或免費升等），回答旅客問題時亦不可以以不知道為由拒絕提供協助，對於尚未掌握的資訊，也需耐心安撫旅客，並告知旅客一有正確消息再主動公布或通知。

前輩經驗巧巧說

一般航空公司遇到機械故障而不得已取消航班，會立即安排旅客的替代航班。若替代航班起飛的時間超過公司一定的標準，會由高階主管下達指示，提供餐點或住宿來慰問，而各航空公司的標準則不同，主管也會視當下情況調整處理方式。

航班取消時，旅客的生氣和擔憂一定會有，重要的是如何有效率地處理。自身遇到的經驗裡，其實旅客生氣發怒的原因就是航班取消帶來的不安與不便，例如情境劇中，Mr.Wang 有極重要的事必須盡可能的準時抵達，或是我曾遇過旅客當次出國是要參加比賽，若因航班取消而晚到會場，會影響甚多，甚至無法參賽。若公司無法提供有效率的服務處理，旅客更加不滿也是人之常情。所以在公司的標準下，盡快達到旅客抵達目的地的需求與安排，往往可以無往不利的解決危機，也可迅速消化旅客的不滿。

4–4 旅客抱怨

情境介紹

一個颱風天，客人擠滿機場大廳。所有人盯著螢幕，想知道飛機到底延誤多久、會不會取消。在 DA 航空的櫃檯前排滿許多提前到機場辦理登機的乘客，每個人都想知道飛機會不會飛、什麼時候飛。

情境對話 Track 39

M ▸ Maggie，**W ▸ Mr. Wong**

W: I am going to Bangkok through DA 687, can I fly today?

M: I am sorry, sir. Your flight is 15:45. There are still 4 hours left, so we cannot confirm with you right now. It depends on the condition of the weather then. It might depart on time or cancel at the last minute.

W: When will the final decision be made? I don't want to waste my time standing here and watching that stupid monitor!

M: Sir, I suggest you take a rest, or find somewhere to have a seat. The situation might change anytime due to the typhoon. I really can't give you the answer now.

W: Uh, have you heard that time is money!?

M: It's for your safety, sir. Airplanes are very fragile and combined with many precision instruments. Above all, this giant transportation carries hundreds of people. This is why we take it so carefully. Please be understanding.

W: How dare you!

M: I am telling a truth, sir. No offence. Whether it flies or not is controlled by the headquarters. Believe me; we are all eager to solve the problem. We have more than two hundreds of passengers waiting for this flight. Oh, we have 7 flights today, by the way.

W: ...Alright! Where is the cafe?! I need an espresso!

M: There is a Starbucks downstairs. Wish you could find a seat. Good luck!

譯文

W: 我搭 DA 687 去曼谷，我今天能飛嗎？

M: 抱歉，先生。您的飛機是 15:45。還有 4 個小時，我們現在無法跟您確認。這取決於屆時的天氣狀況。它可能準時起飛也可能在最後一刻取消。

W: 那什麼時候會有最後結果？我不想浪費時間站在這盯著那愚蠢的螢幕看！

M: 先生，我建議您去休息一下，或是找個位子坐。航班的狀況隨時可能會因為颱風而改變。我現在真的無法給你答案。

W: 呃，你聽過時間就是金錢嗎？！

M: 這是為了您的安全，先生。飛機是非常脆弱的，且是由許多精密儀器組成。最重要的是，這巨大的交通工具承載著數百人。這就是為什麼我們這麼看重這件事。請您諒解。

W: 你好大膽子！

M: 我只是告訴您實話，先生。無意冒犯。它飛不飛是由總部控制。相信我，我們都急切地想解決我們共同的難題。我們有兩百多位乘客在等這班飛機。喔對，順便跟您提一下，我們今天有 7 班飛機。

W: …好啦！咖啡廳在哪？！我要來杯 espresso！

M: 樓下有一家 Starbucks。希望您找得到位子。祝您好運。

英文母語者這麼說

（還有四個小時，我們現在無法跟您確認。）

中式英文：**There are still 4 hours, so we cannot confirm with you right now.**

正確說法：**There are still 4 hours left, so we cannot confirm with you right now.**

雖然中文裡沒有把（to be） left「剩下」講出來，但在英文中，這句話請記得要加上 left，比較不奇怪。另外，原句應該是 There are still 4 hours which is left，但口語中會省略 which is 講起來比較簡單、比較順唷。

字彙解析

- **waste** *v.* 浪費

  This job is wasting my life.（這工作真是浪費我的生命。）

- **stupid** *adj.* 愚蠢的

  Watching fireworks at Taipei 101 is a stupid idea.（去台北 101 看煙火真是個愚蠢的點子。）

- **fragile** *adj.* 脆弱的

  Please put on the fragile tag on this box.（請在這箱子上標上「易碎」的標籤。）

- **precision instrument** 精密儀器

  Digital camera is a kind of precision instrument, so please handle with care.（數位相機是一種精密儀器，所以請小心拿取。）

- **giant** *adj.* 巨大的

  In south-west England, several giant rocks were constructed in an area, called Stonehenge.（在英格蘭西南方有數個巨大的石頭建造在一個區域，叫作巨石陣。）

- **solve** *v.* 解決

  We all want to solve the problem, so please stop yelling at us.（我們都想解決問題，所以拜託別再對我們吼。）

- **eager** *adj.* 渴望的、急切的

  They are eager to eat something.（他們急切的想吃些東西。）

補充片語

❶ on time 準時

例 I will be on time.（我會準時。）

❷ at the last minute 在最後一刻

例 I cancelled my booking of high speed rail at the last minute.（我在最後一刻取消了高鐵的訂位。）

❸ time is money 時間就是金錢

例 My dad told me that time is money.（我爸說時間就是金錢。）

❹ above all 最重要的是

例 Above all, you have taken back the money.（最重要的是，你拿回你的錢了。）

❺ how dare you 你竟敢

例 How dare you do so!?（你竟敢這麼做！？）

解 直接說 How dare you 的時候，可以翻作「你好大的膽子」。

In Other Words

❶ No offence. = Don't be offended.

（無意冒犯。）

解 在討論事情的時候，有時想提出不同的看法，可以先說 No offence, but 表示「別介意」、「不要氣」。

❷ Believe me, we are all eager to solve the problem. = Trust me, we are all eager to find out the solution of the problem that we are both encountering.（相信我，我們都急切地想解決我們共同的難題。）

解 本句用 trust 替代 believe，且使用 find out the solution of the problem 取代了 solve the problem。

地勤工作解說

旅客抱怨的事情很多，想來想去，在台灣最容易遇到抱怨的大概就是颱風天的時候，一整天有接不完的電話、回答不完的問題，更煩的是還沒有辦法給客人明確的答案，因為一切都要聽天由命。這時候就要面對不斷的抱怨，雖然心裡都想說颱風又不是我叫他來的，但還是只能一一跟客人解釋，最後都只能請客人看螢幕，真的也不是地勤人員無能，而是真的無能為力呀。

前輩經驗巧巧說

在機場久了，會抱怨的客人分成發牢騷型及大發飆型兩類。發牢騷型就是邊辦理登機邊碎碎念，綿綿不絕到天邊，此時只要繼續做自己的事，稍微回應他一兩句，也不用解釋太多，他只是想發發牢騷（比方說：上次搭你們家又 delay 啊、飛機上東西怎麼這麼難吃可不可以跟公司講一下啊、超重也抓得太嚴了吧、怎麼又是小飛機啊…），通常講到所有手續都完成，他就會離開櫃台了。最麻煩的就是大發飆型，常常會鬧到要找督導，甚至有直接拍桌的客人，就可以請航警協助，將他請離現場，是可以解決沒錯，但地勤的弱小心靈也是會受到驚嚇的呀。筆者遇過最無理的是一位中國籍領隊，沒頭沒腦對著你大罵，明明你什麼也做錯。好在旁邊同行的台灣導遊，用台語安慰我說，不要理他，他整個禮拜都這樣，就是個神經病。最後送走他的團員後，還買了杯熱咖啡來給我，真是人間處處有溫情啊。

Learn Smart! 056

Ground Crew English

航空地勤的每一天：職場口語英文 (MP3)

作　　者　Stacy Yeh、Joanna Yang
發 行 人　周瑞德
執行總監　齊心瑀
企劃編輯　魏于婷
校　　對　編輯部
封面構成　高鍾琪

圖片來源　www.dreamstime.com
內頁構成　菩薩蠻數位文化有限公司
印　　製　大亞彩色印刷製版股份有限公司
初　　版　2016 年 3 月
定　　價　新台幣 380 元
出　　版　倍斯特出版事業有限公司
電　　話　(02) 2351-2007
傳　　真　(02) 2351-0887
地　　址　100 台北市中正區福州街 1 號 10 樓之 2
E-mail　best.books.service@gmail.com
網　　址　www.bestbookstw.com

港澳地區總經銷　泛華發行代理有限公司
地　　址　香港新界將軍澳工業邨駿昌街 7 號 2 樓
電　　話　(852) 2798-2323
傳　　真　(852) 2796-5471

國家圖書館出版品預行編目資料

Ground Crew English航空地勤的每一天 : 職場口語英文 / Stacy Yeh, Joanna Yang 著. -- 初版. -- 臺北市 : 倍斯特, 2016.03
面 ; 公分. -- (Learn smart! ; 56)
ISBN 978-986-91915-9-3(平裝附光碟片)

1.英語 2.航空勤務員 3.讀本

805.18　　105002286